Whi
Shel
Won
Prom

Ernestine's Story

Karen H

Other Books by Karen Ho

- Shaman Prie
- Down the Co
  Mystery, 1
- Sparrow Hav
- Up the Devil'
        Myste
- The Memoria
  Maggie
- Monster Slay

Children's Book by Karen I

- Little Mouse c
- The True Stor

Intrepid Ink Publishing
Rio Rico Arizona 85648

White Shell Woman's Promise:

The Blessingway is a woman's ceremony
designed to restore order, harmony and beauty.
Its powerful medicine heals those
who participate in the ceremony
from actions and decisions
that might otherwise destroy them.
The Blessingway is done to ensure health, fertility,
long life, and good fortune.
And to restore balance.
The essence of this sacred ceremony
is to build spiritual,
psychological, physical, and
emotional harmony.
The goodness surrounding everyone
is accessible to us
as we live our lives in Beauty.

1

Letter to Wilma

Little Wilma,

I know you're just a toddler and you won't be able to read this for a long time. But I've had the feeling lately that some things can't be put off. Some things have to be said when you're ready to say them because tomorrow may be too late. Tomorrow I might be dead and gone and then how would you know how much I loved you? I need to tell you that I want to be with you forever. I'm your mama and I can't imagine not being here with you and for you, but I have seen so many troubles in my life. It's better if I tell you now how life is.

The people who wrote my story didn't tell how it felt, how I felt. They didn't tell the fear and the hurt. the hate and the sorrow of it all. They were thinking about Grandpa Billy and about Lewis Tsosie and the murders. They needed to stop those men. Those men were evil and they meant to hurt and kill. But they didn't stop to think about all that happened before. They couldn't see into my heart. Nobody could except Grandpa Billy and he's gone. He was good to me, and he was there. He knew. He didn't just hear and think *Oh, yeah, that's too bad*, or *lucky for Ernestine she found a home*. He knew and he cared and he loved us. When I was alone and scared and afraid for you he told me how the Monster's children chose to follow a new path, their own path, to become the eagle and the great horned owl. He told me the Monster couldn't follow me; the choice was mine who I would be.

But the Monster still came in the night into my dreams. Sometimes I fought him all night long and I couldn't sleep. I knew if I closed my eyes he'd be there. That's what monsters do; they steal your peace. And Grandpa Billy knew that too. He talked to me, but he was waiting. It wasn't time yet to do a sing. I think he knew they'd be back. He knew he'd have to protect us again.

And now it's too late.

I'm sorry honey. I had to stop for a few minutes. I can't be letting tears splash down on this letter and smear the things I want you to know.

Anyhow, then Helaman came, and he saw how it was. Helaman took some of the worry off of Billy. He didn't understand most of it, but he saw and he knew enough to walk with me. He made us a family after Billy was gone, and I was whole again

2

Oh, baby. You aren't going to understand all this. I'm going to have to go back to the beginning. I'm going to have to tell you everything. And if we're lucky you'll never have to read this or know about the worst that other people can do. If we're lucky I'll be your mama all your life and Helaman and I will grow old together and you will grow up and marry a good man you can walk beside, and evil won't find you.

But just in case, I want you to know.

2

Beginnings

I was born over near Rough Rock. Well, actually that's not true. I was born in Farmington, New Mexico in the hospital there, the San Juan Regional Medical Center. My mom Betty had a hard time during the pregnancy and the doctor at the clinic told my dad she should go into the hospital when her time came. He drove her over and he brought us home. They were real happy together. Everybody tells me that. They were always real happy.

It took almost three hours just to get to the hospital so I guess they were lucky to make it. There wasn't a medical center in Chinle back then—just a clinic. You would have been born at the clinic or maybe right here in the house if I'd had to make that drive. You didn't wait any three hours to be born. But my momma had time.

They kept her in the hospital for three days before they sent us home. My dad slept in the hospital room. He used to tell me how he slept in a chair that folded out flat, but it had a bar right across his back and he could never get comfortable. He had to stuff his pillows down under his back and then his feet hung off the end. I always imagined him trying to sleep with his cowboy boots sticking out off the end of that chair. He was real tall and skinny. I thought he was the tallest man in the world when I was little. Danny Yazzie. That was his name.

So they were both real glad when it was finally time to go home. And there were three of us on the trip back.

We were all real happy. I remember the house we lived in at a camp south of the highway. I remember the fields my dad planted every year. I remember my mom singing by the stove. You know how those early memories are? They're more like feelings than images and they come in fragments, like broken pieces of mirror. You never have the whole picture, just glimpses, shards of the past. I feel my dad holding me; I smell the fry bread oil smoking on the stove. I feel my mom's breath on my neck when she tucks me into bed and kisses my cheek. And I feel the happiness around me.

Then one day I hear my mom and dad talking, and my mom's crying and my dad's upset. I must have been nearly five. I remember my dad took my mom by the shoulders and turned her around so she had to look at him face to face, and he

5

tells her, "I don't care about the drive, I don't care about the damn chair—I'll sleep on the floor. I care about you and you need to go."

I was little. I didn't understand anything. But my parents were upset and so I was afraid. I ran outside and I hid under the shade house. I pulled my knees up and made myself small. I didn't want trouble to find us. Like you can hide from trouble? I could hear my dad calling me and I put my head down on my knees and I must have fallen asleep. I don't know how long I was out there. I remember waking up when my dad scooped me up off the ground. My mom was already in the car and he just dropped me in the backseat and started driving.

That woke me up good and I leaned forward, but my mom was leaning over holding her stomach and the back of her neck was wet with sweat. I think if I could have seen her face she was covered with sweat and she just kept rocking a little and I knew she couldn't see me or anything else in this world. And my dad, he just looked straight ahead and drove the car faster than it had ever gone before. Finally I looked out the window and watched the sagebrush and the red rock flash past-whoosh, whoosh, whoosh. Everything's flying past my window. And I listened to the sound of the tires on the road until I fell asleep again. Sleep was my escape back then, you see? I didn't know about monsters yet.

3

The Hospital

I woke up when daddy pulled into the parking lot at the Medical Center. I had never been to a city. I had never seen so many cars in one place. I thought the hospital must be the biggest, tallest building in the whole world. But my dad just opened the car door and told me to jump out like it was an ordinary day in an ordinary place. Someday you'll go over to Farmington and you'll laugh at how silly your mama was back then, but you see, I was still little.

My dad went around to the passenger side door and he picked up my mother. He picked her up and carried her. I wanted him to carry me, but I could see that wasn't going to happen, so I ran after him. He was walking fast and now they were both sweating, and I was running, and I was afraid they might forget I was behind them because they were busy concentrating on the building in front of us and getting to the doors.

When we got up to the building the doors opened by themselves with a kind of swoosh. I stopped, I was a little afraid to go through, but my mom and dad walked right in and then the doors started closing so I had to run inside before the doors caught me and I started to cry and I couldn't catch my breath. My dad was talking to a lady and she was bringing a wheelchair for my mom and calling to somebody else and then a man came running and pushed the wheelchair with my mom away, and I never even said good bye. I never imagined she wouldn't be back. But the lady who brought the wheelchair bent down and picked me up and wiped my face with a tissue and told me everything was going to be okay. She was round and soft so I stopped crying and I gulped in air until I could breathe again and then I looked around for my dad. He was sitting in a chair talking to another lady who was typing information into a computer. I walked over and stood by him and he took my hand. He looked real worried and I thought I wasn't going to be able to breathe again, but I was okay.

Then we sat on a bench for a while and every so often my dad would jump up and walk over to the desk and come sit back down. Or he would walk up and down in the waiting room and knock the dust off his hat against the back of his pants until there couldn't have been any more dust on it, but he just kept on walking and knocking his hat until finally a doctor came out and called him.

Then my dad leaned down and told me to stay right there on that bench and not move for any reason. He would come back for me. I didn't want to stay there by myself but I didn't know what else to do. Then the soft lady who held me before came over and she told my dad I could come behind the counter with her and she would look after me.

I remember she said her name was Irene. She brought a blanket and put it on the floor, and she gave me some paper and a pencil and asked me to draw a picture. I drew our sheep and the house with the mesa behind it and I drew me and momma and daddy all standing by the sheep and the sun shining in the sky. I fell asleep again holding that picture of our happy family.

4

Death Comes In

Later I found out my mom was going to have a baby. If everything had gone the way it should have I would have had a baby brother and my dad would have still been happy and who knows what else would have changed. All I can say is life would have been different than it turned out.

But you can't go wishing for that because you still have to deal with life the way it comes, even when it isn't what you hoped for or thought it would be, and sometimes good things do come after all.

But it wasn't until I was ten or eleven that I heard my aunt talking about what happened that day and then when she saw me listening she sat me down and told me the whole story, or at least what she knew.

My parents were real pleased when they found out my mother was pregnant again. My dad wanted a houseful of kids. He wanted his family around him. He said every family created a brand new world; every couple was First Man and First Woman all over again. They had the chance to make a new beginning, a new world of their own. But my mom didn't get pregnant right away.

So they'd been planning and they'd been waiting a long time for this and finally a new baby was coming. My mom must have been about six months pregnant when she started bleeding. She was afraid she was losing the baby. Her mother told her she needed to lay down with her feet up, but my father had a bad feeling. He knew something was wrong. He could see from my mom's color—the color in her face had drained away to gray, and he thought something must really be wrong. Plus she was in pain. Not contractions, just pain, heavy pain, pushing down on her mind and her body. He didn't want to take any chances.

My mom was afraid of the hospital. She wanted to believe everything was going to be okay. Even with the way she felt, she just wanted to go in and put her feet up and wait for everything to get better.

But my father knew. He looked at her and he knew, just as if he'd seen a ghost or glimpsed the future. He knew it was already too late to change things. He put her in the car and then he looked for me. And then he drove into Farmington going ninety miles an hour.

I used to wonder if it was my fault she died. If I hadn't hidden in the shade house would she have been all right? But I know now those few minutes didn't make any difference. My mother was already dead. We just didn't know it yet.

When the doctors finally called my father back they had bad news. They told him that my mom had a cancer on her cervix and they wanted to operate on her right away. They didn't know if it had spread into other parts of the body, but they told my dad the baby couldn't be born naturally and they needed to take it out. There was no question about that. It would be dangerous to take the baby early, but not as dangerous as leaving him inside with that cancer growing up around him.

My dad agreed, but he wanted to be there with his wife when they opened her up. They argued until the doctors finally said okay, and they brought him scrubs and had him wash up and stand up by my mother's side where he held her hand while they put a drape over her and cut open her belly. When they lifted out my little brother he gave a cry and my dad stepped forward and lifted him up out of the doctor's hands. He was tiny and he stretched his arms and legs out into the air, trying as hard as he could to hang on to this world. But his lungs weren't developed and the doctors didn't have any way to save him. My dad held him while he struggled to breath. He held him until he died, and even after when the nurses wanted to take the baby away, he held him.

While my dad was holding his son the doctors were trying to save my mother. The cancer had eaten away at the cervix and the uterus. My aunt had to explain a few things to me that day so I could understand what had happened. You could say that was my introduction to the birds and the bees.

Anyway, the walls of the uterus were like wet tissue paper (or at least that's how she explained it to me) thin and weak. So once the baby was out the uterus tore away in strips. And the doctors were clamping and cutting and trying to stop the bleeding and trying to remove the tumor without leaving cells to migrate into the bloodstream. But in the end they ran out of time. My mom bled to death in the delivery room. No one could anticipate the fragile state of her womb. And it wouldn't have made any difference if they had because even if she had waited, her body couldn't have withstood the labor contractions. They would have torn her apart inside, and she and my little brother would have died anyway.

But my dad? His life was over. All his dreams were tied up with my mom. He sat there for a long time. Finally he had to let go of the baby and he had to watch while they rolled my mother's body out of the room, and then he had to come back out to the admissions office where he found me sleeping with that picture still clutched in my hand.

I hardly remember the funeral. I know you won't remember Grandpa Billy's funeral. You were there but you were still little. My mom's funeral was smaller than Billy's. My mother's parents were there and her sisters and my dad's parents and his brother and sister. They buried her in the ground like we did with Grandpa Billy, with a tiny coffin next to the bigger coffin for my mom. Nobody stayed around for long. We went back to the house and the women cooked and talked and then everybody ate and talked some more, but nobody said anything about my mother. I missed her. I wanted to talk about her. I wanted to know where she was, why she'd left us, but nobody could tell me. Nobody wanted to talk about the dead.

13

After that everything changed. It's funny that things could go along like life was so perfect and turn so ugly just like that. But sometimes life is that way.

5

Daddy

I haven't thought about those days for a long time. After the funeral it was just me and my dad. I missed my mom, but I was glad to be with my dad. He'd sit on the couch and hold me and look out the window for hours. Sometimes he'd talk like we were making plans. Sometimes I felt restless and I would wriggle out of his grasp. Then I walked outside by myself. I threw sticks for the dog. I watched the sky. I walked down to the fields where the corn was dying.

Dad stopped working in the fields; he stopped everything. He just sat on the couch or wandered around the house looking in the rooms and in the cupboards like he'd lost something and couldn't find it. I guess now they'd say he was depressed, but the words didn't mean anything to me. I was lonely, and he was lost. He hardly ever went into the bedroom he and my mom had shared. He didn't want to see she was gone.

A month or two passed and he started drinking. He'd have a beer and then another one. Sometimes when I woke up in the morning he'd be asleep on the couch, empty beer bottles scattered around on the floor where they fell. I picked the bottles up and carried them out to the fifty-gallon drum out back of the house. I learned to find myself something for breakfast and I learned that when my dad woke up he was going to feel stiff and grouchy. Sometimes I walked down the dirt road, kicking my feet in the dust, then cut across the land to my cousins' house. My auntie was always glad to see me and she'd give me something to eat. I could forget the sadness that sat over our house laughing and playing with my cousins until I had to walk back home.

One afternoon we were sitting on the couch watching the clouds move across the sky and suddenly my dad started crying. It scared me and I guess it scared him too. He jumped up and ran out of the house. I ran after him and I was crying, blubbering, "Daddy, daddy, take me with you. Please don't leave me."

He turned around and picked me up. He held me for a minute, gave me a kiss and told me he loved me. It was the last time I ever saw him.

That night I sat at the window waiting for my father to come home. The house felt real empty, real lonely and I heard coyotes off in the distance. I walked around and checked all the doors, turning the locks on the door handles. I wondered if a coyote could come through a locked door. I turned on the TV and sat on the floor waiting. Finally I saw car lights lighting up the front window from down the road. A car was coming toward the house. I was sure it was my dad and when I heard heavy footsteps I ran over and unlocked the door.

There was a policeman standing on the porch. He looked down at me with a real sad face and then he reached out his big hand and took my hand in his and we walked to the police car. I sat in the passenger seat and I didn't say a word. Neither did he. He just backed around and we drove down the road. Back at the station he made some calls. It was past midnight when he drove me over to my grandmother's house. "Where's daddy?" I wanted to know. Grandma just shook her head. She looked old and tired.

"We'll talk in the morning baby girl," she told me. Then she tucked me into a bed with a soft quilt and a soft pillow. "This was your daddy's bed when he was little." She told me.

"I know," I whispered as she turned off the light. But I also knew my daddy wasn't there with me.

I knew my daddy was gone but some time went by before I learned his car had gone off the road at high speed up on highway 160 south of Kayenta. It looked like he had missed a turn at Marsh Pass and the car tumbled ending up at the bottom of a gorge. Nobody knew if it was an accident or if he'd driven off the road there on purpose. Nobody knew if he'd been heading somewhere or just driving. I thought about that last drive with my mom, the car going ninety, the sage brush

17

rushing past the car window. And I thought about the car sailing off the road, over the sage brush, turning and twisting, landing on the rocks, taking him back to my mom.

When my dad jumped up and left the house I was sure he had come up with a big idea and was off to pursue it. I hope he found it.

6

Grandma's House

Grandma told me that bed was mine now so I stayed there with her. I don't even remember going back to the old house for my clothes. But somebody must have gone and cleaned the house, brought out the things we needed, the things we could use. The night after my dad's funeral I went into my room to get ready for bed and there on my pillow was my pink doggy. It was a saggy old stuffed animal, and my mom had said I was getting too big to need pink doggy anymore. She told me she was going to find some tiny baby who could use a soft animal and we would give it to him. But that didn't happen so I was glad to see him there on my bed. I held him all night long telling him the things nobody else could understand.

I knew grandma loved me. She took care of me, she brushed my hair, she fixed our meals, but she never smiled. Thinking back I guess she didn't look forward to starting over again with child rearing. There was that and the loss of her youngest son. Daddy was her last hope. He was married; he was happy, and he'd escaped the monsters of alcohol and poverty that swallow so many of our people. And then just like that he was gone. I was the one left behind. There was a sadness about that house all the years I lived there.

I had to teach myself to be happy. When grandma frowned I smiled. When she sat staring out the window I sang little songs to her and sometimes just to myself. I thought about my parents and I held on to the memories I had of the happy times before everything was lost. I remembered my mom and dad as the happiest people in the world and that's how I wanted to be.

I started school in the fall, not too long after my dad was gone. If he only could have waited he might have been happy watching me go off to school, climbing on the bus, sitting up on the bench seat, waving to him out the window. But he wasn't there.

Going to school helped me. I made friends with all the kids on the bus, but Rachel and Sunshine and Pearl were my best friends. We were all in the same class with the same teacher, Miss Johnson.

Miss Johnson reminded me of my mom and in a funny way that made me feel better too. She spoke in a soft voice and she smiled when she talked. She was slim and pretty and she always dressed up for school even out at our little old building. I looked forward to school every day. I pouted and complained to my grandma on Saturdays and on school holidays for half the year. She just listened to me and told me to go play outside in the sunshine, to run out to the mesa and back so that I would grow up big and strong. And I ran, I ran like the wind my hair flying out behind me that first Saturday. Out by the mesa I found the camp where Sunshine and Pearl lived. Later I found out Rachel lived a little further to the east of us.

Pearl started laughing when she saw me, and pretty soon Sunshine was laughing too. I stomped my foot and asked "What's so funny.?"

"What happened to your braids?" Pearl managed to ask between gasps of laughter.

"My grandma doesn't braid my hair on days when there's no school. She says my head needs a rest or the hair will all stretch and fall out on the ground."

Now Pearl and Sunshine were rolling on the ground laughing and I started laughing too. Pretty soon our skin and hair and clothes were covered with soft red dust. We went over to the water tank and splashed water on our arms and faces until we were covered with muddy red streaks. I leaned into the tank and dropped my arms into the water up past my elbows. The water was almost warm and it felt good. I bent forward to dunk my face in the water and nearly tipped right into the tank. I balanced myself and leaned down so my wild hair was in the water. I opened my eyes and looked around at the murky green underwater world. My cheeks were puffed out and I imagined I was a huge old bullfrog. I moved my arms through the water but my feet were still firmly planted on the ground. I could hear sounds but they were really far away.

21

Suddenly someone started tugging at me. I blew out all my air and stood up straight. Water streamed down my back. I turned and looked at Sunshine and Pearl. "What's the matter?"

"We thought you were drowning in the tank," Pearl sobbed.

I looked at my two friends with their frightened faces and I jumped down and ran over to them. I hugged Pearl and then I hugged Sunshine. Now we were all thoroughly wet and dirty but I didn't care. My friends were worried about me. I told them about turning into a bullfrog swimming under the green water, but they told me to stop talking foolishness. Shape shifting wasn't something to joke about, not even if the shape was just a harmless old frog.

Sunshine tried to braid my wet hair for me without success. The truth is my grandma had arthritis and it was a lot of work for her to braid my hair on school days. I didn't care; I liked my hair hanging down. I liked bending down and shaking it around my face. And I liked being with my friends.

It was the arthritis that kept grandma from her weaving too. She couldn't card and spin the wool into yarn like she'd done her whole life. Her loom sat in the front room by the east-facing window, a beautiful rug about half finished on the loom. But grandma never looked at it and she never talked about it. I wondered if she would teach me to weave, but she couldn't bring herself to face the loom.

Daily life followed the routines of the Rez. At five in the morning grandma got up and stoked the fire. When the house was warm I inched out of the covers while grandma went outside to open the corral and let the sheep out to graze. While I dressed for school, grandma fixed breakfast. We ate together, me in a hurry grandma eating slowly, stretching out the meal,

22

savoring her hot coffee. Before she was finished I was up and out the door, running to catch the school bus.

My friends were always there ahead of me and they called and hooted as I ran up the road. "Hurry up slowpoke. The turtle is faster than you. Come on, you're going to miss the bus. Too bad you don't have wings like Bat. You might have to fly to school." I ran as fast as I could and I never missed the bus.

By the time I was in the third grade our morning routine had changed. Now most mornings I got up and started the fire, and while I went out and shooed the sheep out of the corral grandma got dressed and started breakfast. I hurried inside, breathless, ready to wash up and eat so I could run to the bus with my friends hooting and hollering, urging me on. One thing for sure I had lots of fun with my friends. Sometimes Rachel joined us after school, getting off the bus at our stop so that we could all play together. On Friday nights we would sleep over at Sunshine's or at Pearl's and play together on Saturday mornings.

On Sundays I went to church with my grandmother. She never missed a Sunday meeting no matter how slow she moved in the mornings. Then on Sunday afternoon she sat me down and told me the stories of First Man and First Woman, of Changing Woman and her sister White Shell Woman, and their sons, the Twins. She told me about the days when monster's lived on the earth and how Monster Slayer, one of the twins, tried to rid the world of monsters. She told me about the Flint Boys and on Sunday nights she would point out where they lived up in the sky. She told me how the old world was destroyed by a flood and how the people had to come up through a reed to this world. And she told me about Spider

Woman and how weaving was her gift to women, even thought grandma didn't teach me to weave. I learned so many things on Sunday, listening to my Sunday School teacher in the morning and to grandma in the afternoon. Pretty soon I realized it was all just one big story with different names. In the morning we escaped the flood on the big boat Noah built and in the afternoon we crawled up a reed. In the morning I learned that God put a spirit inside each of us, and in the afternoon I learned that the animals, trees, rocks, and earth had been given spirits as well. One way or the other I learned all the things that mattered.

The school year raced past. The big old cottonwood trees outside the house marked the passing days. When school started the tree was heavy with dark green leaves casting shady splotches across the hot dusty earth. Soon the leaves began to turn until the leaves had changed from green to a bright yellow, trying to hold the sunshine that was now casting less light and heat onto the trees. The tree stayed warm and cheerful as the days grew shorter and cooler.

Then the winds started and the leaves scattered, falling dry and brown across the yard. One morning I looked out at the corral and I saw snow on the split wooden rails. I wanted to crawl back into the covers, but if I did I would miss the bus and school and Miss Johnson, so I walked across the cold floor and pulled on my clothes. We knew it was springtime when the cottonwoods began to turn again, the very tops of the trees turning the faintest, palest color of green. The cottonwoods were the first markers of the changing season, and then before we knew it the cottonwoods were dark green again and the school year was nearly over. Year after year.

One Friday after school we stayed on the bus and went over to Rachel's house. Her father worked in the trading post and he brought videos home almost every night. We watched the *Little Mermaid* and the *Lion King*. Simba and Ariel became our role models showing us how to behave.

That Friday night Mr. Charlie (that was Rachel's dad) brought home the newest video, *Finding Nemo*. I watched Marlin and Coral making a home for their little family. I was mesmerized, glued to the TV, when suddenly the barracuda came and ate Coral. I was stunned What kind of movie was this? Then Nemo hatched out and his father was afraid to let him out of his sight. I jumped up and ran out of the house before my friends could see how upset I was. I hated *Finding Nemo*. I hated the barracuda that ate Nemo's mother.

My friends watched that movie over and over again but I couldn't watched it all the way through. I never laughed at Dory or worried whether Nemo's father would find him. I figured he'd land on the rocks after racing at excessively high speeds down the current. I didn't want to see it. I didn't even want to think about it.

I sat outside until the movie was over and then we roasted hotdogs over a fire and listened to the grown ups talk. Rachel's uncle came in late carrying a case of beer. The men sat and drank and pretty soon they got to arguing, and then Rachel's mom took us inside and tucked us into bed. The next morning after breakfast she drove us home.

At the end of the school year Miss Johnson gave me a kiss on the cheek and told me I was a good girl and she would miss me. When we started second grade Miss Johnson was gone. Mrs. Pete told us Miss Johnson had gotten married right after school was out and moved to Chinle with her husband.

Mrs. Pete was short and round with white hair and glasses that constantly slid down her nose. Sometimes she reached up and pushed them up into place when she wasn't even wearing glasses. She was the opposite of Miss Johnson but I liked her too.

Miss Johnson had taught us the ABC's, but in second grade I got the hang of reading. It was like magic, a whole new world opened up for me. I could open a book and disappear. I could sit in my room and live in another place and time, without once wondering why that barracuda had eaten my mom from the inside out or why my dad had gone away or why my grandma never smiled. From second grade on I was the number one customer at the Bookmobile, standing in line with an armful of books I had already read and leaving with an armful of books to fill the next two weeks. I knew the bookmobile driver by name and he knew me.

When we started junior high we were starting to think about boys. We were taking our lessons on romance from the TV sitcoms. None of the adults thought to talk to us about the things that were really on our minds.

I used my spending money one Saturday in the fall to buy a tube of Ruby Red lipstick. I was sure it would make me the most glamorous thirteen-year-old in Rough Rock. My grandmother took one look at me when I came out of the bathroom and then she held out her hand. I gave her a puzzled look, but she was having none of it. Finally I handed her my beautiful new lipstick and she slipped it into her pocket. Then she sat me down on the couch and she started to talk. She didn't mention the lipstick right away; she started right in with the basics. "You know when Changing Woman created the clans she was really creating families. The family is the center

26

of our life and that's how it's meant to be. Someday you will meet a good man and you will marry him and have children. Do you know how that will happen?"

I thought about it. "I'll meet him at work or at school or maybe with my friends and," I paused. I wasn't sure how we would decide to get married. "How will I know he's the one I will marry? How will he know?"

Grandma almost smiled. "I can't answer that for you. But I can tell you why you'll marry a good man. You're going to marry a good man because you are a good girl who doesn't run around with folks who forgot they have family. You are going to walk and talk and act like a good and traditional woman who knows how to walk in beauty. Now walking in beauty don't mean wearing any of this war paint you been trying to paint your face with. Ernestine you are a beautiful girl—inside and out. Remember that."

Tears popped into my eyes when my grandmother said those words. No one had ever told me I was pretty. My grandmother hardly looked at me, but today it was like she could see into my soul. And she wasn't finished talking.

"Don't you be settling for something that comes in a tube when you got what comes from the gods. You listen to the Yei, you know they're whispering in your ears. You listen and you do what they say. Otherwise you going to only find unhappiness."

She went on, "Ernestine, you are still young, but you are already becoming a woman and you are wondering what to look for in a man. You'll have to watch for the one who is kind, see if he is respectful, if he is traditional. You have to see if he wants a wife and family. Some men wanna drink beer and drive fast and have their way with you without any thought for the family they should be making. They're the wrong ones. They are walking the wrong path, but they will like that bright red lipstick you're wearing. It look like a sign to them saying 'Here I am, take me.' Remember baby, you are worth more than those men can offer. Your beauty don't wipe off with a tissue. You got to wait for that good man who loves you to walk with you in beauty."

I thought about my grandmother's words. "What kind of man was my dad? He drank beer and he drove fast and . . ." I stopped talking. I was afraid of the answers I might hear.

For the first time since I had come to live with her my grandmother reached out and took my hand in hers. "Ernestine, your daddy was a good man. He loved your mother and he loved you. There was nothing in this world he wanted more than a family. After you were born your mother lost three babies. The doctor's didn't look past the miscarriages, but she probably had the sickness growing inside her all that time. Then finally they planted another baby and it was growing and they were the happiest couple in the world. But when your mother died it was like somebody came up behind Danny and hit him over the head with a club. He couldn't see straight, he could hardly walk. His world was broke in pieces."

"But I was still there. I still loved him," I cried out feeling hurt and sad, like a five year old all over again.

My grandmother's voice was deep with anguish. "You loved him baby and he loved you. If he could have just held on until he could see his way again he would have been okay. If he hadn't gone out in the car who knows? But he had lost the way. He didn't mean to go and leave you behind. That was never what he wanted. He shoulda had a healing way, he shoulda; I tried to tell him." Grandma stopped talking and we both sat thinking our thoughts.

Grandma spoke again in a low voice. "No telling what can happen in this life. We got to listen to the winds that whisper in our ears, even when we can's see beauty anywhere."

I nodded and she sat there absently holding my hand lost in thoughts from the past. Finally she stood up. "And don't be thinking those soap operas show the way to walk through this life. Those television shows are nothing but a pack of lies."

I thought about that for a few minutes. Grandma had walked into the kitchen. I walked in and stood beside her. I had a big question now. "Grandma, how did they plant a baby—my mom and my dad? How does that happen?"

My grandmother looked at me and sighed. "Ernestine you are old enough to know these things and you need to know so you don't find yourself in trouble some day." Then she sat down and told me about the birds and the bees, except she actually told me about the sheep and First Man and First Woman and husbands and wives. But she never told me about anyone like Lewis Tsosie, and maybe I wouldn't have believed her if she had. I was only barely thirteen. But at least I knew my parents loved me and even my grandma loved me in her way. I knew important things that some of the girls I saw everyday never learned. I guess nobody talked to them about the reason we live in this big world. So how could they be expected to find their way with all the evil out there wearing Ruby Red lipstick?

One afternoon in the spring we all got off the bus at my stop and started up the dirt road toward the house. We hadn't gone far when Pearl stopped and set her backpack on the ground. She unzipped the top and rifled around inside until she found what she was looking for. She held out her hand. She was holding a packet of cigarettes. "Who wants to smoke the first one?" she asked, her 'I dare you' tone coming through loud and clear. My eyes popped open. My grandma did not smoke or drink. She often told me that smoking and drinking would kill me dead. I thought of my mother who had died of cancer and my father who had had one too many beers before he drove off the road. I thought of my grandmother telling me to stay on the path of beauty. I clamped a hand over my mouth and backed away from the glittering packet in Pearl's hand.

"Ernestine, you are such a chicken," Pearl chortled. "When are you going to grow up?" She slid a cigarette out of the pack and lit it with a flourish, ready to show the rest of us how easy it was. She inhaled a great gasp of smoke straight into her lungs and then she started to cough. Rachel picked up the cigarette and puffed a few times tentatively before passing it to Sunshine. Sunshine inhaled like a pro, blowing the smoke out in a white stream. Her parents were both smokers. "There. That's how it's done," she stated matter-of-factly. "Now put that foolishness away." She dropped the cigarette in the dirt and stomped it out with the toe of her shoe. Then she turned to Pearl. "Pearl, cigarettes aren't cool."

I exhaled the air I had been holding in my lungs, afraid to breathe, and that was the end of our smoking days.

We were the lucky ones. No cigarettes, no pot, no alcohol. That first small step kept us from going further down a dark path.

30

7

High School

I continued to attend church with my grandma but even
in the pew listening to the 'good news' she rarely smiled. She
would inspect my dress and hair and nails and once in a long
while she told me I looked nice. She fixed me meals, she woke
me up in time to catch the school bus, but she did all those
things without a show of affection. I knew she loved me. I
thought of the day we had sat talking and she had taken my
hand and once in awhile sitting next to her in church I would
put my hand on hers. I wanted her to feel the way I had felt
that day.

I asked her one day why she never smiled. She looked at me and answered, "My teeth bother me." Then she paused, "I have seen too much unhappiness in my life."

"What about the happiness you've seen?" I asked.

"That's what makes it so hard," she replied. I didn't ask her again.

But I saw happiness all around me. I saw it in the tiny flowers that managed to push up out of the sand, the clouds, the sunny days, the occasional sprinkling of snow on the mesas, the stars sparkling in the night sky, the sparks from the fire. All of it made me smile.

Pearl, Rachel and Sunshine started ninth grade with me. We still rode the bus together, we sat at the same table in the cafeteria, we laughed at each other's jokes and listened to each other's heartaches. It made being in high school easy.

8

The Enemy Way

In July before the start of our senior year Sunshine invited me to an Enemy Way ceremony with her family over by Baby Rocks. Her uncle had gotten out of the army a few months earlier. I guess he'd done his share of fighting and he'd spent three years living the military way. He wanted to live the Navajo Way. Sunshine's mother and brothers were going. I asked my grandmother for permission to go and she agreed. She was hoping I would learn the Navajo stories. She started explaining the Enemy Way ceremony to me, telling me about the warrior, and about the war camp, and especially about the dance, and how if I snagged a polite young man I shouldn't let him go until he'd paid a good price. It was one of the few times I saw her smile.

I was real excited. It was my first ceremony and I looked forward to it, especially the girl dance at the end. The Enemy Way dance was the way young women found a husband back even before my grandparents got married. Now it was the way young women met young men.

We didn't date. We had friends, we hung out together, but we didn't date. Even if a guy liked me what was he going to do? Pick me up and take me to a movie? Go out to dinner? Come over and sit on the porch with me and my grandmother? But it didn't matter; we were almost seniors. The future lay open before us.

The girl dance is a war dance, but it's also a courtship dance. I wanted to meet a nice guy. I wanted to be part of the circle. I wanted to dance, to meet a boy, to talk and laugh. We were going to have a good time.

On the ride out to Baby Rocks Sunshine, Pearl and I sat in the back of the pick up truck. Black Mesa loomed in the distance big and dark. Red sandstone cliffs capped with white Navajo sandstone stood like guardians at the side of the highway. Red sand hills interspersed with rough black cliffs marked our way. Pinion and juniper grew up the sides of steep buttes and their pungent odor filled the air. We hardly noticed it. It was the view we saw everyday on our way to school.

We were bouncing along in the truck bed laughing, talking about the fun we'd have. The sun shone down on us and the wind blew past. We scrunched up against the back of the cab but we were as light as the wind. We could have been flying above the bed of that old truck. It was a wonderful, light, happy feeling that we all shared and it stayed with us when we set up camp.

We stayed in the enemy camp down the road from the hogan where Sunshine's uncle was doing the sing. We helped fix food. We helped prepare the men for the second day battle. We walked over and watched when Sunshine's uncle Samuel came out of the hogan at dawn and vomited all the evil out of his system. I wondered if I could just throw up the evil that had come into my life when I was small or if my grandmother could be cured, if she could learn to smile again. I decided that I would have to do in without a ceremony, with my friends around me. The things that had happened to me were just life.

Watching uncle Samuel, sweating, bent over and holding his knees, retching and coughing, I couldn't imagine the evil that was about to reach out and knock me to the ground when I didn't even know I was in danger.

9

The Dance

We spent most of the last afternoon getting ready for the dance. We braided each other's hair. We added barrettes, ribbons, clips, turquoise—and then we undid it all and started over. Sunshine had a make-up kit. We shared lipsticks, mascara, blush, and eye shadow. We had to keep it subtle or Sunshine's mother would make us wash it all off. We tried on clothes, swapped outfits, and finally we were ready. Sunshine's mother and aunt looked us over and declared us the prettiest girls at the Sing. We were satisfied.

The first few girls were mosstly shy, stepping forward toward the light, then looking away. But their mothers stood behind them, encouraging them, pushing them forward, out of the nest. A girl approached a man standing guarded in the midst of his friends. The girl linked her right arm through his, and facing away she pulled him into the circle. She had captured her man. They danced with the pulsing of the drums and the chanting, up and down, around the circle, around the fire blazing in the center feeling the heat.

I stand with Sunshine and Pearl and Rachel. Sunshine's mother and her aunt stand behind us. They whisper to us, pointing with their lips toward eligible looking young men. We giggle, they giggle with us. Finally Sunshine's mother pushes her forward away from the group. She looks back her face half smile, half grimace. Then she straightens her shoulders and walks over toward a group of young men. Soon she is out in the circle.

The girl selects and the girl leads. The man follows. Always. It is lady's night at the War dance. A man, the captive must pay to leave the dance, but payment in jewelry and horses has given way to an exchange of money. And it has to be an acceptable offer. If it is too little the dance continues and the man follows. The circle fills with couples, moving forward and back, everyone in motion. Sunshine and her man dance in the circle, focused on the beating drums, their moving feet. He isn't trying to get away.

Those outside the circle may laugh and joke, point and gossip. But the dancers don't crack a smile. The dance is part of the ceremony. It is serious business. And on the third night the business is dancing and collecting, dancing and paying. Or for a lucky few, dancing and finding each other.

Soon Rachel and then Pearl move forward. Tentatively I follow. I link arms with a young man. He seems shy. He gives me a half smile, I smile back and we move into the circle. This is it. The circle of life and I am a part of it. The bonfire blazes high and we feel the heat. My young man is named Jonathon Willie. He is from Tsegi Canyon. His family knows uncle Samuel's family and they came down together to participate in the sing. But a lot of his friends are here just for the dancing. Eventually we make our way over to the edge of the dancers. We are both panting. Jonathon laughs and talks. I laugh and respond. But his friends call to him, heckle him and finally he lifts a bolo tie with a turquoise stone over his head and places it around my neck. "Can I call you, Ernestine?"

I smile. "Of course." He writes my number on his hand. He doesn't know when he'll be in Rough Rock. But we had fun. We part smiling.

My throat is parched. I look around for something to drink. There is a tub filled with ice-cold sodas. I walk over to the tub. I don't see any of my friends. It's darker away from the circle and the bonfire. Others come over to grab something to drink. There is jostling for position. I move back from my spot near the tub. I bump into a man in the crowd. He spills his drink. I turn and apologize. He laughs. His name is Lewis Tsosie.

10

Lewis Tsosie

We stood and talked. The night was warm but breezy. Lewis looked down at his shirt. "I need to change my shirt," he said and smiled pulling the soda drenched fabric away from his skin. "I have a clean shirt out in my truck. Why don't you walk out with me and then maybe you can ask me to dance?"

I laughed. "Maybe I will, maybe I won't. You know I'm going to have to make up my mind on that while we walk over to your truck and back." Our mood was light. I was happy.

We walked away from the crowd and the light. We walked past most of the cars and trucks but Lewis said his truck was further out. It was dark now. Lewis took hold of my elbow and guided me across the churned dirt of the parking area. As we got to the edge of the parking the dusty air seemed to clear. The noise of the dancing seemed far away. I looked up at him. How much further? He smiled. "It's right here." There ahead of us at the furthest edge of the parking lot was his pick-up truck. He walked over and opened the passenger door. He unbuttoned his shirt and I turned my head. He tossed the shirt into the truck, reached in and pulled out a clean shirt. He pulled on the shirt but didn't button it up. Instead he reached back behind the seat and pulled out a six-pack of beer. He popped the tab on a can and handed it to me. I shook my head. "Sorry, I don't drink." Lewis shrugged and chugged down the beer. He popped open a second can.

"Hey Lewis, I think I'll head back to the dance." I was starting to feel uncomfortable.

He nodded. "Hang on, I'll walk back with you." He held out the half full can of beer. "Hold this while I button my shirt."

I took the warm can and held it out in front of me. Lewis moved over behind me, talking, buttoning his shirt. He reached over my shoulder to take the beer. I started to turn and he wrapped his arm around my neck, holding me in the crook of his elbow.

I started to laugh. I was suddenly nervous and it occurred to me that those weren't the first beers Lewis had drunk that night. "Hey Lewis, you've got it backwards. I'm supposed to capture you," I joked.

Lewis didn't laugh. He pulled me back against him and pushed his hand up under my shirt. It was so unexpected I

40

reacted without thinking, jabbing my elbow back into his ribs. "Stop that. Let go of me. I'm going back over by the fire." I pulled away and he pulled me back.

Now I was afraid. I had been so naïve walking out across the dark parking lot with a stranger and it never occurred to me that it might not be a good idea. I struggled, trying to pull away, but Lewis was bigger than me and stronger. And he knew what he was after. He held my wrist, bending it so that I cried out in pain. He reached forward and slapped me hard across the face. I was stunned by the physical pain. "Shut up," he hissed hitting me with his fists. I kicked and bit but he ignored my efforts to break away. He grabbed the front of the blouse I had borrowed from Pearl, the blouse I had so carefully chosen that afternoon. The buttons popped off as he pulled the front of the shirt open.

"Stop it! What is the matter with you?" I screamed

Lewis pulled me around and stared at me but he didn't see me. He pushed me down and I scraped my back against the short stonewall marking the edge of the parking area. I struggled, trying to stand, trying to move away from Lewis, but now his full weight was on me pushing me over on top of the rock wall, keeping me off balance. I cried out once more, but he clamped his hand over my mouth, and he held me with the weight of his body. I heard the sound of his belt slithering against the denim of his pants as he pulled it off. I was crying, gasping for air, my face in the dirt. I put one hand down holding my upper body up off the ground. I wasn't sure what was coming. Well, I had some idea. We had all taken health class, but I had never imagined this.

Suddenly I felt the warm, sweaty leather of his belt against my neck. Lewis looped the belt and tightened it around my throat half choking me. He kept tension on the belt ready to tighten it more. "I told you to shut up. You make a sound I will pull this belt tight." I felt like a dog on a choke chain; I felt lost, trapped, stupid for being where I was.

Lewis didn't waste a lot of time talking. He pushed up my skirt tearing it; my dance moccasins were ruined. It's funny the things you think of when your life is in danger. I concentrated on my beautiful beaded moccasins, scuffed and dirty. I could hardly breath. I tried to pull myself away reaching and pushing against the edge of the stone wall. My fingernails were broken, my mascara was smeared but Lewis stayed with me. His pants were down around his knees. I could feel his skin against me, his weight pushing my head down. I thought I was going to die. I wanted to die.

11

Monster Slayer

Suddenly I heard a bellow, a loud voice. I couldn't see who was there but I could hear his words. "I am Monster Slayer, Naayee neizghani. I am here to slay this man." The voice was full of power. I craned my neck so he could see the terror in my face; he could smell the alcohol and smoke rising from the body of the man who held me down. Lewis turned to look as the man ran forward. Then he dropped the end of his belt and pulled at the front of his pants as he ran toward Monster Slayer. But Monster Slayer stepped aside and the monster flew past him just as it happened in the stories my grandmother told me on Sundays.

I turned, pulling my blouse around me and holding the edges together. I felt shaky, wobbly. Monster Slayer was an old, old man. But he stood facing Lewis. He turned when Lewis moved, catching his breath and watching that evil man. He could hear the wind whispering in his ears. I listened too and the wind seemed to say to me "Be still, don't move; you will be alright." But I was full of fear and despair for myself and for the old man. Lewis came back toward the man. He held a knife in his hand. I called out but Monster Slayer had already seen the knife. He picked up a big rock and held it behind his back. He allowed the evil man to come close, to reach out for him even as I screamed out in fear. When Lewis was very close the old man lifted the rock and brought it down with all his strength on Lewis's head. When Lewis stumbled, Monster Slayer grabbed his knife, the blade clearly visible in the moonlight. He held it in front of him and told Lewis to leave. The evil man stumbled and turned away, leaving his blood on Monster Slayer's hands and chest.

Suddenly the old man felt weak. His hands shook, his knees shook. He wobbled over to where I was standing unable to move. He could see that my face was swollen, that my cheekbone was broken. He dropped to his knees beside me and spoke soothing words, "Do not worry. I will protect you. He cannot hurt you anymore." I looked at the old man kneeling beside me, speaking words of comfort and I realized he could not stand. He had used his last ounce of energy to defend me.

Tears spilled down my face, making tracks across the red dirt. "He will come back. I have been warned of his kind before. Why was I so blind? He is evil. He will not allow us to live." I was terrified. "Am I still a good girl?" As the old man tried to comfort me I felt my strength give way, my knees refused to hold my weight and I sank down beside him.

"Don't worry, daughter. I am here with you." The old man spoke softly, "I have his knife. He cannot trouble us again. We will talk to the police." I could hear his voice growing weaker. He sank lower to the ground. I leaned against him unable to move, to stand, or run for help. Tears fell from my eyes and I lacked even the strength to stop them.

I needed to go for help but I felt so weak, so tired. I could not leave the old man alone. He had saved my life. I leaned against him feeling the pain in my cheek, my neck, my knees, inside me. I should have felt relief, maybe even elation at being saved, but all I felt was pain and shame. I couldn't have felt worse if I had been thrown into the bonfire. No, in the bonfire I would have felt better—the pain would have been clean. As I sat next to the old man thinking my thoughts his strength and goodness overcame me and I fell asleep.

When Uncle John found us his father was leaning against a low stonewall, apparently sound asleep. I was huddled next to him, gripping his arm.

That was how I met Grandpa Billy.

I don't remember much of what happened after that. John must have lifted us both into his truck and driven straight to the Indian Health Service Hospital in Kayenta twenty some miles away. John was nearly incoherent as he tried to fill out the paperwork at Admissions. He didn't know what had happened. He had no idea who I was or where I'd come from. He had no idea what had happened to me or to his father. He had all the necessary information for his father Billy Gray Eyes

45

except for what he was doing on the outer edge of the parking area, how he had gotten hurt, and what his connection was to me, an unidentified young woman. I must have looked a mess. My blouse was ripped open; my skirt was torn. I was covered with the thick red dirt from the parking lot, my face was swollen and streaked with tears and mud, I was bruised and bleeding. At that moment I didn't look like a carefree young woman about to start her senior year of high school.

The admissions clerk pursed her lips and shook her head as she entered information into the computer. When the report was as complete as John could make it she asked him to wait in a side office. The tribal police were on their way to the Health Center.

Billy was treated for shock, dehydration, and low blood sugar. He was otherwise healthy. The blood on his hands, arms and chest belonged to someone else. When he was pronounced well enough to go home he was taken into custody and charged with assault and rape. The police would be looking for the man he had attacked.

John was furious. "Didn't you hear what my father said? Did you listen to one word of what happened? My father is a respected hatathli, he didn't hurt that girl."

The tribal police shook their heads. "You really think your old man was capable of stopping a much younger man? You believe his story?"

John had his doubts about some aspects of his father's story, but he had no doubt at all that his father had not assaulted and raped a young woman, then fallen asleep with her holding onto his arm. I don't remember any of this. I was under heavy sedation, being treated for trauma to the head and neck, a crushed cheekbone, not to mention other injuries. It was several days before they dropped the levels on the sedatives and I was coherent enough to be interviewed.

In the meantime Billy Gray Eyes sat in a cell in Kayenta thinking about what had happened to him. The stories of his youth became very real once again, the power of the ceremonies and of the Sings coursed through his veins. They could keep him in a cell, but they could not take away the things he knew; they could not take away his power.

I remember the day the police finally came in to see me. They wanted to know about the old man, what he had done, how he had overpowered me. I was outraged. I now understood what it meant to add insult to injury. I had been injured. Billy Gray Eyes had also been injured saving my life. I told the police about Lewis Tsosie. I told them about bumping into him at the Sing, spilling his drink down the front of his shirt, walking out to his truck so he could find a clean shirt. I told them how naïve and stupid I felt. I told them how Lewis had taken off his shirt, drunk a couple of beers and attacked me. I told the police that Lewis Tsosie was a Monster and that Billy Gray Eyes was a great hatathli, and that I had seen him turn into Monster Slayer with my own eyes.

The police wanted details. I told them how Lewis had ripped my clothing, forced himself on me, put his belt around my neck to control me and maybe to kill me when he was finished. I told them how he had pulled the belt tighter when I tried to fight him off. I reached up and rubbed my neck where the leather had burned the skin. And I cried. I cried as I relived the horror of that night; I cried as I felt the relief of being safe and alive.

The police made their report and sent me back home to my grandmother in Rough Rocks. I got up in the morning and opened the corral, watching the sheep spread out across the grassy flats behind our house. I fixed breakfast for my grandmother and me, but I felt weak and tired. I had been through an ordeal. It would take time to regain my strength.

Then I started throwing up. I couldn't face breakfast. I had no appetite. My grandmother watched me and frowned. "You need to let this go child." That was her advice to me. I needed to let it go. But I didn't know how to let it go. It wasn't the assault that had hold of me now. It was something inside me.

School started. I ran for the bus. Sunshine and Pearl and Rachel were already there waiting. They didn't call out to me to hurry. We were seniors now, too sophisticated to yell and laugh and roll on the ground. Sunshine sat next to me. She looked at me, and her face tightened. "Ernestine, you don't look so good. Your color is terrible. Are you sure you're alright?"

What could I say? I was sure I wasn't all right at all.

On the way home Pearl sat beside me. "Ernestine, we all know something terrible happened to you, but please, try to find your smile again." She turned her face away. "When things were bad for the rest of us you always kept your smile. You kept us all going. Look at us. We're seniors. We're going to graduate. We're going to college. You never let us give up, and we don't want you to give up."

I nodded, mute. My stomach turned over and I thought I might throw up right there on the bus. I tried to smile, but tears slipped out of my eyes. Pearl leaned over and embraced me. We sat like that together for several minutes. Then we straightened up and I sat looking out the window seeing nothing as the bus moved down the road.

I couldn't sleep at night. I had dreams—nightmares. I knew what that word meant now. I was back with my mother and father. I dreamed of the barracuda that had eaten my mother, of the pain that had killed my father and I dreamed of the Monster who was stealing my life one breath at a time.

My grandmother started getting up early in the mornings and letting the sheep out. I was like a little child again. I needed to get up, I wanted to go out and do the morning chores, but my body felt heavy. It refused to obey the messages I sent to my feet and legs and arms. One morning early I got up to go to the bathroom. I wobbled in and sat on the toilet. Suddenly it struck me; I hadn't had a period for more than three months, not since that night. I stared down at the water in the toilet then leaned over and vomited.

I turned away from the toilet and turned on the shower. I stood under the spray until the water turned cold, letting the water run into my mouth, through my hair, and down my body. I scrubbed my skin with soap, then scrubbed it again. I washed my hair and let the shampoo slide down my skin, but I could not wash away the darkness that had entered my soul.

At breakfast I tried to talk to my grandmother. "Grandma, something's wrong. I need help. I need to see a doctor." She turned her face away from me. "Grandma, I can't go to school today. I am not well."

Grandma stood up and cleared her place from the table to the sink. "Go to school Ernestine. Go catch the bus. The doctor can not cure you." She would not look at me; she had no answers to give me. I dressed slowly. It seemed as if my body resisted the movements I made as I tried to pull on my Wrangler's and shirt. I leaned down to tie my shoes and nearly fell. When I sat back up I was dizzy. I walked out the front door, looking back at my grandmother's stoic, unhappy face. I walked up the road, one foot in front of the other. I knew I had missed the bus, but for the first time in twelve years the bus was late. I climbed up the steps and took the first seat in the front. I stumbled off the bus in front of the school and walked to the nurse's office.

When the nurse, Mrs. Whitehorse, came in she could see I was not well. She took my temperature and my pulse. She asked me what I'd eaten for breakfast. I mumbled at her, "I think I'm pregnant."

The nurse looked at me in surprise. She didn't know. "Ernestine, have you been sexually active?"

"No!" I wanted to scream, *I haven't been sexually active. I was raped. I don't even know what sexual activity is but I have a monster child growing inside me.* Fear filled me and I began to sob.

The nurse walked out. When she came back in she was all business. She must have talked to somebody who knew. Who didn't know? Who could I look at who didn't see the girl who was raped? The girl who had no sense? The girl who walked out in the dark with a stranger? Now the nurse's face was tight. "Why do you think you're pregnant? It isn't very likely that one encounter would result in pregnancy."

I looked at the middle-aged woman in the white lab coat, her hair cut in a short bob. She was educated. She was non-traditional. She was a nurse, but she couldn't look at me when she talked. She couldn't use the word rape. No, she had to say "one encounter" like I had bumped into somebody in the trading post. And I was just as bad. I couldn't say what needed to be said either.

Finally the nurse determined that I had not had a period

50

since that "one encounter." I told her I felt so nauseous and dizzy almost every day that I couldn't eat.

"It could be stress Ernestine. All your symptoms could be caused by simple stress."

There was nothing simple about my stress. Who would ever say simple stress? Stress isn't simple. But I could feel the life inside me. I know it was too early, but I knew.

After half an hour of mumbled conversation and embarrassment on both sides Mrs. Whitehorse agreed I should be seen by a doctor. "Maybe it would be better if you don't go here to the clinic. You might want to keep this somewhat private. People can be unkind."

I thought of Sunshine and Pearl and Rachel. I thought of my grandmother and my classmates. Three friends. Only three who would listen and understand maybe, what I was feeling. I nodded. Mrs. Whitehorse went back into the office for just a minute or two then came back walking briskly. "Come on Ernestine. I'll drive you into Chinle myself."

We didn't talk much as we drove the thirty some miles into Chinle. I looked out the window. Mrs. Whitehorse commented on the weather; it was lovely September weather. Soon fall would be here. I thought of the cottonwood trees, the leaves turning yellow, then brown and blowing away. Fall would come and winter and there would be nothing left. I would be like one of those leaves. No more Ernestine.

12

The Clinic

It's funny when I thought about Lewis Tsosie I never thought about the future, or about justice or retribution. It didn't occur to me that he was a wanted man. It didn't even occur to me that I might run into him again somewhere. He existed only in that one moment of time when he had torn me from my world.

We walked into the clinic in Chinle together and Mrs. Whitehorse spoke to the woman at the front desk. The woman, whose nametag read Clarice, frowned and shook her head, then began turning through the pages of a scheduling book. Mrs. Whitehorse spoke to her again, pointing to me and tapping the counter. Finally the woman got up and walked into the back out of sight. When she came back out she sat down and wrote my name in the book and said to have a seat; someone would see me in a few minutes.

Ten minutes later I was in an examination room. The nurse had me undress and put on a robe. She weighed me, took my blood pressure, had me pee in a cup and took blood out of my arm. Then she left me sitting on the end of an examination table. Eventually a woman came in. She introduced herself as Doctor Peterson. She was young and tall and blonde. Her eyes were sky blue. She wore a white lab coat and had a stethoscope around her neck.

"I'm going to need to do an internal examination Ernestine." Her voice was light, almost musical The only internal examination I had had previously was after the assault over at the clinic in Kayenta. I had been in pain and the examination had been extremely uncomfortable. I could feel my body tense. Dr. Peterson talked to me during the examination. "Try to relax Ernestine. This will take just a minute. There's your cervix. Good. Okay, I can feel the uterus. You're doing just fine. How do you like Rough Rock? How did it get its name? No, I've never been up that way. I graduated from University of Arizona Med School down in Tucson. Yes. Have you ever been to Tucson? Well it's a lovely area—hot in the summers though. No, I moved out here from Pennsylvania. I'm doing my year of community service. It is so beautiful here. You are very healthy Ernestine. Do you run track at school? No? Well, I think you're going to have an easy pregnancy. Congratulations by the way . . . ."

So it was true. Dr. Peterson chattered on unaware of the agony that had reached in and twisted my heart, strangling me so that I could not respond to the lovely young doctor's questions. I was pregnant. My dreams of college lay shattered around me. I wasn't even sure I could return to high school.

How could this be happening? Why had it happened to me? I held back the tears until I was dressed and back in the car with Mrs. Whitehorse. What would my grandmother say? She was too old to raise a child. I know because that's what she told me from time to time. How would she respond to news of a baby? My thoughts were dark on the drive back to school.

It seemed like I had been gone for days but school was just getting out as we pulled into the parking lot. Mrs. Whitehorse gave me an awkward hug and whispered, "Don't worry, things will work out."

I wondered what she could possibly mean by that as I ran to catch the bus home.

Sunshine and I walked from the bus to the turn off to her family's camp. "Are you okay Ernestine? I didn't see you in chemistry today. Hey Charlie John asked me if I thought you would go with him to the Harvest Dance next month." Sunshine giggled. "He's kinda cute, don't you think? I told him he should ask you."

I nodded my thoughts elsewhere. It was work just keeping my feet moving forward down the dusty dirt road. I could see my grandmother's house in the distance. Grandma was sitting out in front of the house when I walked up. Mrs. Whitehorse had called before we left for Chinle. She must have called her again with my news. She looked up at me, the hands in her lap twisting one way and then the other, her mouth pulled down in a frown.

"Ernestine, what am I going to do with you? I'm thinking maybe you should go over and stay with my daughter Shirley."

Shirley was my dad's sister. She had a houseful of kids and no husband. She lived over at Inscription House on the road up to Page. "Why would I go over to Shirley's?"

"She knows about having babies and she could use some help now that Sherman's up and left her."

"What about you, grandma? How are you going to get along? Who's going to make sure you're okay, that you're not lonely?"

"Don't you be worrying about me. I am an old woman and I have years of practice taking care of myself. Now go inside and pack your stuff."

I was stunned. "But what about my friends? What about saying good-bye to Sunshine and Pearl and Rachel? What about my classes? I need to check out of school. I need to . . ."

Grandma cut me off. "You need to go pack your stuff. Ronald is on his way. He'll give you a ride over to Shirley's place. She's expecting you." She didn't wait for my reply; she turned and walked inside.

I packed my clothes, my schoolbooks, my drawings, my make-up and hair clips. I packed my treasures, little things from my friends, and finally on top of it all I put my old pink doggie. You know pink doggie—he sleeps with you now. It didn't make a very big pile, which was just as well. I knew I wouldn't have a lot of space at Shirley's house. I had hardly finished emptying drawers and the closet when I heard Ronald honking out front. I had folded my things and placed them neatly into a black trash bag. Ronald grabbed the bag and

55

tossed it into the back of the pick-up truck. I stopped and gave grandma a hug and told her I loved her. She pursed her lips indicating the truck and gave me a little push. As we were pulling away she raised one hand and waved good-bye.

13

Inscription House

Shirley's house was small and rundown. She came out and watched as I lifted the trash bag filled with my life's belongings and lugged it up to the front door. She smiled and reached out to give me a hug. "It's good to see you Ernestine. You're going to have a really good time here. Come on in and I'll show you your room." She turned in the doorway and smiled at Ronald. "Now don't go running off Ronald. I'll be right back out."

She showed me a small bedroom with two twin beds and a crib. You can sleep in here with Merry and Sue Ann. We'll just move Sue Ann back into the crib. She looked around the room. There should be room for your stuff in the closet. Maybe you should pull those sheets off; Sue Ann still wets the bed. You can just toss them in the washing machine out back." With that she turned and went out front to flirt with Ronald before he could jump back in his truck and escape.

It was nearly October. I thought about everything I'd be missing back at the high school—the Halloween Carnival, the Harvest Dance, Thanksgiving break and the build up to Christmas. But I had other things to think about now.

When Shirley came inside I asked her about school. She shrugged. "Why don't you just get on the bus in the morning and see if you can start classes at the high school here."

When I got on the bus in the morning I had no idea where it would take me. We headed down Indian Route 98 toward Highway 160, but I was surprised when the bus driver turned off on a secondary road and headed back to the northeast. The bus finally stopped at Shonto Preparatory School, twenty miles from Aunt Shirley's front door.

I stood in front of the school and watched students stream past. Shonto? I was in Shonto. I knew from the time I had spent in the hospital in Kayenta and from the many interviews with the tribal police that Billy Gray Eyes, the old and well-respected hatathli who had saved my life, lived in Shonto. I was overcome. I felt the wind rushing past my ears, a wind that made me feel dizzy, nearly pushing me to the ground. And in that wind I heard my future. "Go find Billy Gray Eyes. He will know what to do about this baby inside you." I can tell you now, that in that moment the spirits turned me around and put me on the path I should walk.

I suddenly felt confident. I knew where I was going. I walked into the front office and asked the school secretary if she could tell me where Billy Gray Eyes lived. She looked me over and asked me what I needed. "Billy is my grandfather," I replied, confidence in my voice. "I need to find him. His sister sent me over here but her directions weren't clear."

The secretary shrugged. It was a busy time of morning for her. "Look, Mr. Gray Eyes lives out to the northwest. Elementary bus 67 is going that way. Tell the bus driver Iris told you to ask him for a lift. He can point out the house and he'll drop you off."

Some things are meant to be. Me finding Billy again was one of those things. I found bus 67 and boarded with confidence. Orville Nakai just shrugged when I delivered my message. "Okay, sit right here behind me so I don't forget." Orville drove his route picking up his young students. Finally he pointed out a house sitting back from the road. A tall cottonwood filled the front yard, its leaves nearly all on the ground. I looked at the house, the pick-up truck parked on the north side, and I stood and got off the bus. I knocked on the door and then I stepped back to wait. I was not expected or invited. But I knew this was where I belonged.

Neither Billy nor I knew at the time that that same week over in Teec Nos Pas two tribal police officers arrested Lewis Tsosie for the assault and rape of a minor. By Thanksgiving Lewis would be incarcerated, given the maximum sentence permitted by Tribal Law, two years in prison at Chinle Correctional.

59

14

Monster's Child

Standing outside the door I started to feel nervous. When Billy opened the door his face lit up. He smiled and reached out taking my hand. "Ernestine, how good to see you. Come in. What brings you to visit a lonely old man like me?" He chuckled as he said the words so that I would know he was making a joke about being old and lonely. I knew he was old anyway.

"I came to thank you for saving my life Mr. Gray Eyes," I began.

He looked at me his eyes searching, cutting to my innermost secrets. "You look good Ernestine, much better. How have you fared? Have you found harmony again?"

I shook my head, "No." I felt tears welling, trying to spill out of my eyes. I turned away and dried my eyes with the backs of my hands. "Mr. Gray Eyes . . ."

"Call me Billy, daughter. You are here in my heart. Not a day goes by that I do not think of you and hope you are finding your way."

"Billy I need to talk to you. I have a problem and I don't know what to do. I can't sleep. I can't concentrate. The monster comes into my dreams. But there is something else, something I don't know how to talk about, not even with my best friends."

Billy looked at me and he noted the color in my cheeks caused by the increased blood supply of pregnancy—that glow expectant women are said to have. He stepped back from the door. "Ernestine come in and sit down. Let me get you something to drink. You must be thirsty."

I sank down into the softness of Billy's old sofa. I sipped the cool drink Billy brought me and I let myself relax for the first time in many days. Billy watched the tension leave my body, saw me relax in the dim light of the living room. He waited for me to speak. The time stretched out. Neither one of us was in a hurry to be anywhere. Finally I felt the strength I needed and began to talk. "You remember what happened?

I waited for him to respond. I had lived with the assault every day since it happened. But maybe for Billy it was already old news, history. But no. He nodded, he remembered. "I went to the doctor yesterday in Chinle. I am pregnant. I am carrying the child of a monster. What will happen to me? What will happen to us? Will this baby be evil?"

Billy listened to my fears and then he began to speak. First he asked me how I came to be in Shonto. I told him about my grandmother and about packing up and coming over to Aunt Shirley's. I told him about Aunt Shirley, about taking the school bus from Inscription House to the Shonto Prep School, and how standing in front of the school the little winds had whispered to me telling me to find Billy and now here I was.

Billy nodded and then he told me the story of Monster Slayer and the Rock Monster Eagle. My grandmother had told me parts of this story but now Billy changed the focus of the story. He talked about Rock Monster Eagle's children born on the top of Shiprock. He told how after he killed Rock Monster Eagle, Monster Slayer made the children swear to change their ways of being and help the people. The children were not like their father. They were able to change. The first became Golden Eagle and the second became Great Horned Owl "Don't worry Ernestine. Your baby is not a monster. Each of us can choose who we become. She will be your daughter, I will be her father. She will learn the Navajo Way. The monster is dead to us. He cannot harm your child."

I wish I'd known then what I know now. I wish Lewis Tsosie had really been dead that day. But he is dead now and he seemed dead to us then.

Billy looked at me and he saw a young woman, young and alone. Billy told me to wait until the baby came to make any decisions. The baby would help me know what I should do. "Your baby will be a blessing to you," he reassured me.

He offered to let me stay at his house; I could use his son's old bedroom. He showed me through the house. I was reluctant to accept his offer; it was too much. But he repeated it; I could stay with him. He would be my father and I would not be alone. I was torn. What would my grandmother say? What would Shirley say? But the little winds tickled my ears whispering, "This is home." And in my heart I knew this was where I belonged. It was what I needed and what I wanted.. The yei had brought me to Billy's door and so I agreed to stay.

Still I had some concerns. What about Shirley? What about my grandmother? Billy reassured me. He would talk to Shirley, and he did. Shirley I think was indifferent. Billy explained to her that I needed to be closer to the school, that the bus ride every day might not be good for me. Shirley shrugged, "What am I going to tell my mother?" Billy smiled. "Don't worry I will speak to Ernestine's grandmother. Everything will be all right."

And it was.

Billy imagined you growing as a young Golden Eagle or perhaps as a Great Owl. When he first saw you after you were born he clapped his hands together, staring down and whispering, "Yes, a golden child." But he never imagined you would someday carry his name, the name of the humble medicine man, Billy Gray Eyes. Little Billie, when you hear your name remember your grandfather.

15

Home

That first afternoon Billy went to see Shirley. He told me they had a nice chat and he retrieved my trash bag filled with the few things I could call my own. As I was getting settled in the bedroom I heard voices in the kitchen. I put down the things I was arranging and walked out to meet whoever it was at the house. If this was home I couldn't hide out in a back room.

Billy introduced me to his grandson Delbert, explaining that he was my cousin. But in fact Delbert became the little brother I almost had. He wasn't quite eight years old, but he was a serious boy, ready to study and learn the Navajo Way from his grandfather. Someday Delbert will be a great hatathli. But back then he was just a little boy who loved Grandpa Billy as much as I did.

Billy and I talked about school. It was almost October and I was due to have a baby in April. Maybe it wasn't the best idea to register for school in Shonto. I was a senior and I wanted to graduate, but the more I thought about it the more I saw that I wouldn't be walking with my friends, I would be stepping into new classes with new teachers who didn't know me or what I could do. Billy suggested I take the GED and then he helped me sign up for the tests. I passed the tests without any difficulty and that was that. I was finished with high school. It felt good and it felt strange at the same time. I wanted to call Sunshine and brag a little, but then there would be all the other things I hadn't shared with my friends and didn't plan to talk about. I didn't make that call. Instead I set to work becoming part of the Gray Eyes family and to my surprise, Billy's sons accepted me as their little sister. I worried about John. He'd seen me at my worst, the dirty, incoherent girl he had taken to Kayenta along with his father. But when he came to pick up Delbert that first evening he smiled and welcomed me in to the family. "Dad needs somebody to look after him and put a little spring back in his step. You keep him busy Ernestine." Then he leaned down close to my ear, "You look real good. I'm glad you're doing better. We worried about you." I could feel tears trying to find their way to the surface, but I put on a smile and thanked him for his concern. The only thing I could figure was that the winds must have whispered in his ears too and he must be the type of man who listened. I had a family, and that was something to cry about. Now I understood tears of happiness.

Me, the girl who had always loved school, suddenly found myself moving to new rhythms. I got up early and watched the sunrise. I fixed breakfast and planned lunch and dinner. I made shopping lists. I played with the dog, throwing hundreds of sticks for the little dog to fetch and bring back to me. I read books and in the afternoons when Delbert came over I sat and listened to the stories Billy told. Billy told stories and then he talked about what they meant, and why they were important for us now. He taught Delbert ceremonial chants and Delbert memorized them, sometimes taking notes to help him study. I stood at the sink washing dishes or peeling potatoes just so I could listen in on the teachings Delbert seemed to absorb like water.

And my baby grew. I watched my body change. I jumped the first time the baby moved inside me, stopping Billy and Delbert mid-story with my news. Delbert laughed and threw his arms around my middle putting his ear against my belly. Finally he pulled away and gave a happy shrug. "Next time maybe." I reached out and gave him a hug of my own before he sat back down and began reciting the sing he was learning.

One morning as I raked the yard, bringing all the leaves into a pile, I looked up and noticed the faint green at the top of the cottonwood tree. I smiled. It was almost time. I'd been living at Billy's for going on five months. I had begun to heal physically and emotionally. I was starting to smile again.

I woke up real early on Wednesday morning, before it was light outside. I could see the gray color the sky gets before sunrise, gravely moving from black to gray to pale purple before the first streaks of gold broke the horizon.

I felt restless. My back ached. I got back in bed and stretched and rolled over on my side trying to get comfortable. I needed to pee, but when I waddled into the bathroom nothing much happened. Finally I got up and went into the kitchen. I drank a glass of water and sat watching the sunrise. It was a beautiful, golden morning.

Billy came out and stood looking at me. "I think your baby's coming today, Ernestine."

I looked up in surprise. "I haven't had any contractions, just this backache." I rocked a little in my chair.

Billy chuckled. "Sometimes that's how it starts. Let's go into town and get you checked."

When we went into Kayenta for our monthly grocery run I usually drove, but today Billy insisted on driving. By the time we reached Marsh Pass in Tsegi Canyon where my father had driven off the road, I was glad I wasn't behind the wheel. The backache had reached around and become a series of contractions. Billy handed me a pocket watch and told me to count out the contractions and tell him how long it was before the next one hit. The counting and timing kept me busy. It was six minutes between one contraction and the next, then four. Suddenly the contractions were coming every three minutes, but it felt like they were comingright on top of each other to me. Billy watched me and talked and I watched the road between contractions, feeling nervous, hoping we'd make it in one piece to Kayenta. He herded that old truck down the road like it could find the way by itself while he was busy worrying about me.

He talked to keep me from worrying. When he was born, he told me, his parents were out working the sheep. His father put his mother into the back of their wagon and headed for the hogan. Halfway home she called out for her husband to stop. She could go no further in the bumpy wagon bed. She climbed down and went off behind a juniper tree where she squatted and delivered her baby. Billy's father waited with the horses. When his wife finally came back carrying Billy in her arms her husband admired his new son then helped his wife back into the wagon bed and took them both home.

"Of course I took my wife to the clinic when our children came. She wasn't going to give birth out behind a tree. Ways change. Now you're going into a hospital. But the babies come all the same."

I looked over at Billy. I'm glad to know you and your mom survived ecause if we don't get to Kayenta soon I'm afraid I'm going to end up having this baby on the side of the road. If it's a boy I'll name him Billy cause he was born just like you. I grimaced and Billy put his foot down on the gas pedal. We made the forty-five mile drive in just over an hour.

You were born on March twenty-third at ten thirty in the morning. I checked you all over and sure enough you were perfect, just like Billy promised. I think you look a little bit like me. Seeing you for the first time was one of the sweetest moments of my life. You came with a little cap of black hair and your nose was squashed flat. I was worried I had an ugly baby, but pretty quick your head rounded out and your nose took its place right where it belongs on your face.

Visitors started coming in to see you. First John and his wife Lucy came by with Delbert. Then Albert and his wife stopped in. Pretty soon Daniel and Jacob came by. They all wanted to see the new baby. They all wanted to introduce their kids to the new sister-cousin. If there was anything that convinced me the Gray Eyes were my true family it was the love my brothers showed me when you were born. Even after we came home Lucy and the other wives came over every day, bringing food and baby clothes and blankets, and trinkets they knew we would need.

One day I found Delbert down on the floor tickling you under the chin, making funny faces, jumping back and forth like an old crow. "What'cha doing Delbert?" I asked him and then it hit me. "You're tying to capture Little Billie's first laugh."

Delbert looked up at me, sheepish. "I'm just playing," he insisted.

"Yeah? Well you keep clowning around and she's going to laugh for sure." Delbert smiled at me and then he smiled at you, and on cue, you started laughing. I clapped my hands and Delbert jumped up and ran circles around the room. chanting "Little Billie laughed, she's here to stay!"

16

Extended Family

Six weeks after Wilma was born Billy surprised me by buying a little car. He drove his old pick-up everywhere and seemed attached to it. I couldn't imagine him in a little compact. Then he really surprised me by handing me the car keys. "You need to be able to get around. That pick-up truck of mine is hard to drive—no power steering, bad brakes, big steering wheel, a stiff clutch. You need both feet and both hands to drive my truck. I can't have you driving Little Billie around in that old thing. It won't do at all." That little car turned out to be a wonderful gift, allowing me to go to school over in Page, giving me the freedom to explore and a sense of independence. I spent that year taking care of you, my little daughter, learning to be a mother, cooking, washing, cleaning, telling stories, singing, and laughing. Summer passed, fall came again, then winter and in March we celebrated your first birthday. Soon summer approached again.

At the end of May we drove to Kaibito to visit Billy's sister, Alberta. Her grandson Mo was coming for a visit and the family used the opportunity to have a get-together. That was the first time I met Helaman, but I don't remember him from that day. The next day Mo and his friend Nicky Thomas drove over to Shonto with Helaman tagging along. They wanted to talk to Billy about doing an Enemy Way Ceremony. The Enemy Way is only done in the summer so they would be busy if Billy agreed to be their hatathli. I remembered the Enemy Way Ceremony from two summers back. I felt my throat constrict, my breathing grow shallow. But I had decided not to live in the past. I looked at you, sound asleep on the couch and I worked to breathe normally, to slow my heartbeat, to listen and participate in the conversation with these members of our family.

And what a conversation it was. Nicky didn't talk much. She smiled and she had a nice smile but Mo and Billy talked mostly in Navajo. I smiled at Nicky, but I really wanted to listen to Billy and Mo. I wondered why a bellagana woman would want an Enemy Way Ceremony. Evidently Billy had some of the same questions.

He asked Mo. "Tell me grandson, why you want an Enemy Way grandson and be specific. I need to understand everything. But first clarify something. Does this young

71

bellagana woman also want an Enemy Way Ceremony? I will need to know some very specific things about her and about your relationship to her before I make a decision. A wife often participates in the ceremony with her husband, but this Nicky Thomas is not your wife." Billy inclined his head toward Nicky as he spoke those words. I looked over at Helaman and he looked back at me, rolling his eyes as if to ask, "What is my big brother up to?"

Mo began telling Billy about the cases he and Nicky had worked on over the last two years as FBI agents. He talked about murder committed by a man named Yag Hosain. He explained how they tracked the evil man. He talked about the huge explosion that destroyed Glen Canyon Dam and Yag's role in that act.

Billy was well aware of the destruction at the dam and its effect locally. He hadn't realized that the Colorado River, a sacred river given its red color by Changing Woman herself, had spread its floodwaters through the lowlands all the way to the Sea of Cortez. "Maybe White Shell Woman made it so," he mused. "White Shell Woman is guardian of the water."

I listened and wondered about the things I was hearing, but I did not interrupt. *Could the gods us the act of an evil man to wash away an evil,* I wondered?

Billy continued talking, thinking now about the dam and its effects on the river. "After the dams were put in the river often ran clear. Even the river had forgotten its origins."

Mo shook his head, "Grandfather, the destruction caused the deaths of many thousands of people even far from the dam itself. It caused a loss of power and water in areas where many people live in cities and depend on power and water for life."

72

What a silly statement. People everywhere depend on water for life. We could not live here on the reservation without water. But we knew it was a precious commodity and we had learned not to waste it.

Mo talked about a sniper. Billy wasn't sure exactly what a sniper was. Mo searched for words to convey what a sniper did. "Remember the warrior, K'aa K'ehi, the *Man like a Shooting Arrow*? Remember how he shot the arrow through the center of the target in Bosque Redondo? He shot an arrow that freed our people. A sniper is one who can shoot with great skill and accuracy, one who shoots to stop evil."

I smiled at this explanation. Mo understood his grandfather well enough to know that using our stories was the best way to reach understanding.

Billy nodded thoughtfully. "Of course I remember K'aa K'ehi, the hero. But a man who can shoot with great skill and accuracy may choose to use his skill on the path of beauty or in the way of evil."

"That is true grandfather, but when the sniper killed this man Yag, he killed an evil man, an enemy of our People. One of Yag's people shot Nicky Thomas. She spent many days in the hospital."

I glanced over at Nicky and mouthed: "You were shot?" She nodded but didn't speak.

Billy looked at Nicky with new appreciation. "Why was this young woman in the path of danger?" He asked.

"Nicky went to find one of the men who helped destroy the dam. Others opened fire. Nicky was hit but she returned fire and she killed one of the men."

Billy was somber. "I am sorry Mo that she had to fight an evil enemy. Perhaps we can talk to her about the Enemy

Way. There are evils that can be removed from the mind and heart no other way."

Mo nodded, but he was not finished. He talked about the dangers they had faced in Los Angeles in stopping a terrorist cell, then continued with a brief account of their trip to Mexico in pursuit of those responsible for bringing dangerous substances into the United States. Mo told his grandfather of the many men killed there and of their hurried drive back to the U S border.

Billy frowned, his old face furrowed with deep wrinkles. "You have been busy. Both of you have been busy. You have been exposed to great evils just as you said. You have taken evil into your minds and hearts. Thus it happens. It is good that you came to me now. Today is Friday. Can you be ready for your Enemy Way by Wednesday?"

Mo smiled with surprise and relief. Not only had Billy agreed to do the Ceremony, he wanted to do it immediately, with only a few days to prepare. "Yes grandfather. I will be ready."

"I know you will be, but there is a great deal we must teach this woman before Wednesday. You must come in the afternoons. I am teaching Delbert, and I will teach Nicky Thomas the things she needs to know for the Enemy Way at the same time. Delbert needs to learn the Enemy Way anyway."

I was astonished. Billy was inviting a bellagana into the house to learn one of our most sacred ceremonies. I would be doing a lot of dishes and peeling many potatoes while her instruction was underway. I was curious to hear what Billy would share, what he would teach this woman with the long

74

blonde hair. I looked over at Helaman once more to see if I was the only one surprised by this turn of affairs. He looked at me and shrugged his shoulders. It certainly sounded like she needed a healing.

Mo was talking again, "We'll be back this afternoon. When should we come?"

"When you see the school bus you will know Delbert is on his way." Billy waved his hand as if clocks and schedules meant nothing to him. But I remembered him handing me his watch to keep track of my contractions and I almost laughed out loud.

"One more thing. You must speak to Nicky. She must agree to be your wife. I cannot do a Sing for her otherwise."

"I was planning to speak to her after the Ceremony, when we are in harmony once again," Mo stammered.

So the FBI agent wasn't invincible.

Billy simply looked at Mo. "Well, plan to speak to her today. I need to know she will be your wife when you come back this afternoon."

Mo and Nicky stood up to leave. Helaman looked over at me. It was obvious Mo didn't need Helaman's help during the next few hours. I stood up and stretched. I was stiff from sitting. I walked over and shook hands with Nicky and Mo. "Well, I need to hang clothes on the line," I announced. "Can't let wet clothes sit too long." I smiled at Helaman and he stood up on cue.

"Mo, Nicky, I think I'll stay and help Ernestine. You two can surely get along without me for a few hours. I'll be here when you get back."

I walked through the kitchen and started loading wet laundry into a basket. Helaman followed and carried the

75

basket out to the clothesline in the backyard. I carried Little Billie out and set her down under the clothesline. We faced each other hanging clothes, pinning them onto the line with the clothespins, talking together about Mo and Nicky and the war they had been involved in. It was over that clothesline that Helaman and I became friends.

When the clothes were all hung out to dry we sat on the bench under the cottonwood tree. Helaman told me he was studying up in Page. I told him I had gotten my GED and I hoped to go to school in the fall, but Page seemed a long ways away. Helaman talked about growing up in Kaibito and going to school in Page, living in town during the school year. I talked about going to school in Rough Rock and watching my grandmother's sheep. Our conversation was easy and natural. It didn't replace my conversations with Sunshine, Pearl, and Rachel. They seemed so far away now. But talking to Helaman wasn't girl talk. It was better.

When Mo and Nicky came back smiling and holding hands I realized I hadn't thought about my first Enemy Way at all after those first few minutes. The thought made me smile. The past couldn't reach out and control me. That's what I told myself on that sunny summer day.

17

Defeating the Enemy

Billy was ready. Nicky and Mo were ready. A second hatathli was in place to oversee the "enemy" camp. Food was prepared. Gifts were arranged. They couldn't have been more ready if they had had a month to prepare. Wednesday and Thursday were busy. Friday morning Billy lay down in the hogan and took a nap, with instructions to wake him up before noon. The battle between camps starts at midday and he had to be there. I was amazed at his stamina. I was amazed at Mo and Nicky's stamina. The battle between camps went as scheduled, gifts were exchanged. At sundown the Women's War Dance would begin. I stayed close to members of the family, laughing and joking with Mo's younger sisters, talking with Lucy and Luanne. The beating of the drums filled the air. The light and heat from the bonfire reached skyward. I watched as young women chose their man and entered the circle. I watched the dancing from the sidelines, bouncing my little daughter to the beat of the drums and the stamping of feet when I felt a tap on my shoulder. I turned and there stood Mo's sister Emma. She held out her arms for you and pointed with her chin toward her brother Helaman. "Take pity on my brother. I don't think anyone here is going to ask him to dance."

She laughed, I laughed. Then I walked over and hooked my arm through Helaman's pulling him into the circle. Hoz'ho. Harmony. Beauty. That is what we strive for in this life.

Of course we all attended Mo and Nicky's wedding in Kaibito in early September. Somehow Nicky looked Navajo to me now, even if she was in the bellagana clan, but it was funny to see her mom and sister preparing corn cake. But even that slipped into the realm of harmony as the day went by. I wondered if someday I too would marry. Would I meet a man who could love me? Would we have children, your brothers and sisters? I was almost nineteen but marriage seemed a long way off for me, maybe even impossible.

As I stood thinking my deep thoughts Helaman walked up carrying two plates of food. "Wanna eat with me?" I held out my hand for one of the plates, my deep thoughts evaporating like summer rain. We stood side by side eating and talking. We finished our food and moved closer to the hogan where well-wishers were giving advice to the newlyweds. Everyone seemed to speak a mix of English and Navajo making sure Mo's wife understood the advice they shared. Suddenly Mo stepped over and put a hand of Helaman's shoulder.

"What are you doing little brother? You can't borrow the advice the old ones give me and my wife. You've got to get with it and ask this girl to marry you. Then you can listen to advice of your own."

Helaman laughed. "I don't know what you're talking about." But he did and so did I. I blushed standing there in the moonlight. Mo could see what we didn't see yet, that we were more than good friends, more than cousins.

18

School Days

I looked at the cottonwood tree and shook my head in disbelief. The leaves were on the ground. It had been two years since I came to Billy's house, since I came home. Thanksgiving and Christmas were just around the corner. You were walking and talking, ready to be twenty months old on Thanksgiving Day. I smile to think I have an almost two-year old daughter.

I'd started the nursing program at Coconino College over in Page that fall and was well into my first semester. It made for long days, but coming home, hearing your tiny footsteps running toward the door, your voice surprisingly loud calling my name, "Mommy!" made the day seem suddenly short. I scooped you up for a hug and you followed me around the house. You followed me in the evening just the way you followed Billy in the morning and Delbert in the afternoon. We had things worked out pretty well here in our safe little world. I was born to be your mom. Delbert was born to be a hatathli and Billy was born to show us the way.

We celebrated Thanksgiving with Alberta's family. This year we decided to be the Indians at the feast. It was nice to have a few days off from school. Then suddenly the semester was over and we were off for the Christmas holiday. We spent Christmas day with Billy's sons and their families. I don't think you remember your first Christmas. But the second one was incredible. You were lost in paper, tissue paper and ribbons. You hardly noticed the presents. And there were cousins everywhere. Lucy pulled me in with the other women and we made food and more food. What a great holiday—presents, good food, and good conversation. Even now after everything, I smile thinking of that day.

Then it was January and I was back in class, starting the second semester. I drove over to Kaibito and met Helaman at the Spirit gas station just off the highway. He drove from Kaibito into Page. I left my little car behind the station. Helaman said he was driving over for classes anyway. I could save gas and he'd have company. It was a great arrangement.

Classes were going well. I was doing well and having a good time. Helaman is such a joker that riding to school together was never dull. He was finishing the third year of a four-year degree. I was finishing the first year of a two year program with the possibility of moving into the four year track.

Everything was just about perfect. I got up early on Wednesday morning, the tenth of February. I'll never forget that day. Our classes started late on Wednesdays so I didn't have to be in Kaibito until ll:30 or so. That meant we got to play nearly all morning. Billy was trying to fix a loom that had belonged to his wife. He thought maybe Lucy could teach me to weave when I had some spare time. He was going to teach me to be a traditional woman.

Just before 11:00 I kissed you good-bye, asked Billy if he needed anything from town, and turned toward the front door. For some reason that morning I stopped and walked back. I thought of my grandmother, how she was always telling me she was too old to raise a child, and here I was leaving you with Billy, an eighty-two year old man. At that moment I was overwhelmed by all he did for us. I walked back and patted his arm and thanked him. He took my hand and told me he loved me. He had always wanted a daughter. He told me I was a blessing to him. Can you believe that? After everything he did for us, when I tried to thank him, he ended up thanking me.

He didn't mention the strange car he'd seen driving past the house earlier in the morning.

19

Dark Wind

I pulled up behind the Spirit Station and was locking the car just as Helaman pulled up. He waved to me and I ran over and climbed into the passenger seat.

Helaman held up a hand, "Before you start telling me what new and amazing things Little Billie did this morning I have to pump gas. So hang on to your stories for five minutes."

I laughed. It was true. I started our commute every day with news about my favorite baby. Helaman pulled up to the gas tank, but before he got out of the car I managed to say, "It's not Little Billie I was gonna talk about today, it's Grandpa Billy."

Helaman saw my smile, knew there was no cause for alarm and turned as he got out of the car, "Hold that thought." He pumped the gas and went inside to pay.

But Helaman was alarmed when he came back to the car. I was sitting with my shoulder against the passenger door, my head down, my hand across my face, trying to disappear. "Ernestine, what's the matter?" Helaman reached over and physically turned me toward him. My face was tight and my breathing was shallow. I could feel my heart racing. It was all I could do not to scream out loud.

Instead I whispered. "I think I saw a ghost. That man, the one who was right here next to us, he looks like the man who . . . you know, the man that Billy stopped when . . . " I stopped talking unsure how to continue.

Helaman pulled me over next to him on the seat and put his arms around me. There was worry in his voice. "You think you saw Lewis Tsosie? He's in jail, Ernestine. We'll know when he's released. He doesn't know where you are and I won't let anybody hurt you."

His words were brave, but I knew what I'd seen.

"I don't know Helaman. It looked like him. I don't know. It's been almost three years; I saw him in bad light back then, but when I saw that man pumping gas I felt cold. It was him."

Now Helaman started to worry. "Did he see you?"

"Nope, he never even looked my way."

"Hey, Ernestine, breathe. I'm going to take care of things; I'm going to take care of you. When we get to Page I'll call Chinle Correctional and find out what Tsosie's status is. If he's out we'll call Billy and tell him to be careful. But I think the last thing Tsosie would want is to do is over here looking for trouble."

I could feel myself shivering against Helaman's shoulder. Maybe he was right. Lewis Tsosie had no idea where I lived. It wasn't like we were in Shonto. We were on the main road into Page. If the man I saw was Tsosie, and that was a big if—if he was Lewis he could be headed anywhere.

Helaman turned up the car heater, pulled out of the gas station and headed to Page. He made the drive in record time, pulled into a parking spot on campus, and we ran to the computer lab where he found a phone number for the Chinle Correctional Facility. He punched it in to his cell phone. A woman answered, and Helaman asked, "Excuse me, I need to know the status of an inmate in your facility."

"Name?"

"Lewis Tsosie"

"You're Lewis Tsosie?"

No, ma'am. I'm trying to learn the status of Lewis Tsosie."

"I'll need your name."

Helaman gave his name, "Helaman Black." He was beginning to feel impatient.

"What is your relationship to Mr. Tsosie?"

"I am not related to him ma'am. I just want to know whether he's been released or is still in custody."

"I am sorry Mr. Black. We do not give out information on our inmates unless there is a family relationship or a need to know."

"I need to know. I am with the young woman he raped. She thinks she just saw him at a gas station."

85

"The young woman is with you? Can she verify her name and date of birth and authorize you to speak on her behalf?"

"Yes. Sure. Here she is." Helaman handed the phone to me and I told the woman who I was then handed the phone back to Helaman. I could feel my heart start to pound. It was like I could feel Lewis Tsosie's presence across the airwaves.

The woman put Helaman on hold while she looked up the information.

Helaman walked up and down the aisles in the computer lab waiting for the woman to come back on the phone. After what seemed like an hour but was actually four minutes the woman was back. "Sir? Mr. Tsosie was released November twentieth of last year—Yes, that's right, two months ago. No, we do not know where he is at the moment. We do not keep a record of his whereabouts after his release. Of course. He may have a probation officer. Do you want me to check? Well okay. Good-bye."

Helaman looked at me. "What do you think we should do?"

"Call Billy." It was all I could think of. Tsosie was up to something. I couldn't think of a single reason why he'd be here, but I was sure Billy needed to know.

Helaman agreed. He punched in Billy's number and listened to the phone ring. He was about to disconnect when Billy picked up on the other end.

"Billy, this is Helaman, Helaman Black." Helaman kept the speaker on so I could hear the conversation.

"I know who you are Helaman. Is everything okay?"

"I don't know, but when we stopped for gas in Kaibito Ernestine saw Lewis Tsosie at the gas station."

86

"Yeah? What kind of car was he driving?" What kind of a question was that?

"I think it was an older Chevy sedan, kind of gray blue. Why?"

"He drove out here earlier—drove around the house and then took the back road out to the highway."

"You saw Tsosie?"

No. I saw a gray blue sedan. I don't get a lot of traffic past the house. I looked out my front window to see who was driving around."

"What do you think he's doing?"

"I think he was checking out the area. He'll be back."

"Billy, I'm heading to your place right now. You need to get out of the house. Do you have somebody you can call?"

"Listen to me Helaman. You're nearly two hours away. There isn't time to call anyone. I have little Billie here at the house and Delbert is going to show up any minute. I'm not going anywhere. Tell Ernestine her daughter is safe and keep her away from the house. Do you understand me?"

"No Billy. You need to get out of there."

"Son, I am eighty-two years old. I am an old man. And I still have some dignity. I am not going to go running up the road with a baby; I'd be putting little Billie's life in danger. I can't carry her far and if I put her down she's likely to run away from me. I won't let that excuse for a Navajo chase me out of my house." Billy was quiet. Helaman almost thought he had hung up, then he spoke again, "Helaman, look after Ernestine for me."

The phone disconnected. We turned and ran for the car. I realize now Billy could have taken his old truck. He could have waited for Delbert at the bus stop or called any one of his sons, but he was protecting me. He knew Lewis wouldn't be satisfied with an empty house. He would keep coming back until he got what he wanted. Billy figured if Lewis took his revenge on an old man who'd bested him on the field of battle he would go away and leave the rest of us alone. He stayed so Lewis wouldn't find me. He stayed so he wouldn't find us.

20

Murder

After hanging up the phone Billy walked over and took his old double barrel shotgun out of the closet. He reached up for a box of shells and loaded the gun. Then he pulled on his winter coat and dropped a handful of shells in his pocket. Finally he leaned down and talked to Delbert who had just come in the back door.

Later Delbert told me what he knew, what he'd seen. Billy told him an evil man was coming to the house; Delbert was not to go outside under any circumstances. "You must protect little Billie. No matter what you hear or see you must make sure the man doesn't see you or Billie. She cannot protect herself. That is your job today." Delbert said he knew something was really wrong. He was scared but he followed Billy's instructions. "Delbert, your job is to protect your little sister-cousin. Sing the Blessingway to her. She must stay quiet no matter what happens. Remember the things I've taught you. I am an old man; evil cannot hurt me. I will go outside the house. Do not follow me. Do you understand? Stay in the house."

Billy walked outside and sat down on the wooden plank bench near the cottonwood tree. He leaned his back against the tree and thought of his wife Danita; he thought of his sons and his many grandchildren. Only Delbert had studied the Navajo Way and he still had so much to learn. He had only scratched the surface. He thought of his daughter Ernestine and little Billie—you and me. He had us there in his heart.

He had lived a good life, God had blessed him, and he knew he would see Danita again shortly. He reminded himself that death is a part of life. He did not fear the chindi, he was old and evil spirits would not mar his death, but still he would not die inside the house. He didn't want anybody to decide this house should be abandoned.

He sang softly to himself, "Father, give me the light of your mind, that my mind may be strong; Give me some of your strength, that my arm may be strong . . ." His mind was off in the past when the sound of a car coming up the dirt road brought him back to his present situation. The car slowed as it turned south, then pulled on up the road in front of the house. There was Lewis just as he had expected.

As Lewis got out of the car Billy stood up. Another evil

90

man, a man Lewis had met in prison was in the car with him, but he rolled out of the backseat as Lewis made the turn south. Now that bad man, a man who didn't know Billy, who had no grudge against him, crept up toward the north side of the house on foot.

Billy spoke in a loud voice, startling Lewis. "Did you learn nothing? Why do you come to the house of an old man? You are like a child without family, without relatives, without respect or understanding. Go away, get back in your car and go now while you can still walk through this world with your head up."

Lewis's head snapped around at the sound of the voice from over by the tree. He saw Billy standing, apparently unafraid.

Lewis carried a large rock in his jacket pocket "I thought you were Monster Slayer," he called back in a mocking voice. "Now I see you are only a weak old man."

"I thought you were a dog, and now I see I was right," Billy replied. He didn't know another man stood by the corner of the house unseen, watching for blood.

Lewis screamed as he moved toward Billy. His evil friend moved forward at the same time. Billy saw the movement from the corner of his eye. He was surprised Lewis had brought someone with him. He picked up his shotgun from behind the tree and turned, facing Leon. "So it takes two of you to come after one old man. You are even less than I suspected." Lewis looked at his friend and then ran toward Billy screaming. Billy turned back to Lewis raising the shotgun and firing, but he had no time to aim. The shot was wild. Pellets sprayed Lewis's cheek and shoulder but most flew past him. Lewis pulled the heavy rock from his pocket and knocked

Billy to the ground bringing the rock down on Billy's head. Billy felt an intense pain, but the rock came down again and again until he felt nothing at all.

I wasn't there but the memory of those moments lives in my mind. I see what happened as clearly as if I had been standing at the window. Delbert heard the blast of the shotgun. He crept up and peeked out the window in time to see the skinny man hit your grandfather again and again. He wanted to go out and help Grandpa Billy, he wanted to scream at the skinny man, but he remembered his grandfather's words. He had to protect Wilma. He ran back into the bedroom and covered you with a blanket hiding you in your crib. He stood near the door waiting for the monster to come, and making sure the doors were securely locked. When I think of Delbert inside the house I remember waiting for my father, locking the doors so the coyote couldn't come inside.

Delbert watched the car drive away then ran to the kitchen, picked up the phone, and called his father. John called the tribal police before running to his car. Helaman and I pulled up just after John got to the house. John was in the front yard. He'd covered his father's body with a blanket. He was sitting under the cottonwood tree, his head in his hands. Delbert was sitting beside him, leaning against his father. I think Delbert was in shock. We probably all were.

When I was five years old I thought the worst thing that would ever happen to me in this world was the death of my parents. When I was seventeen I believed there could be nothing worse than being assaulted, hurt, and raped by an evil man. But when I saw Grandpa Billy brutally murdered and lying dead in his front yard I willed my heart to stop beating. How could I go on living with Billy laying there dead and cold.

We should have called sooner, driven faster. I should have been here to save Billy the way he saved me.

21

And they killed the dog too

An ambulance transported Billy's body to the coroner's office. John picked up Delbert holding him like an infant against his chest. I held Little Billie, watching as John put Delbert into his pick-up truck and backed out of the yard being careful not to drive past the north end of the house. He'd come back to bury the little sheep dog Lewis's friend had killed.

Helaman called his parents. Joseph and Esther talked to Alberta. She was agitated and wanted to head straight to Shonto. And she wanted Joseph to call Mo. "We need the FBI on this. We need justice."

I thought about Alberta's words. Was it possible that Lewis Tsosie would be arrested again and serve at the most another two years for this murder? He was a dangerous man, a vicious man. Alberta's words echoed in my mind. *We need justice.* We needed justice we couldn't get in the tribal courts.

Mo and Nicky flew in on Thursday morning. As soon as they arrived Alberta sat them down for a serious discussion on what had to be done. "Why was Lewis Tsosie only given a two year sentence for assault, rape, and attempted murder?" she started out, her frustration clear in her voice.

Mo waited to make sure she was finished speaking. Then he waited a few more minutes for courtesy's sake before responding. "Grandmother, I know you are frustrated with reservation justice. We all are. You know the reservations are under Federal jurisdiction. The FBI is the agency authorized to enforce the law and bring to trial and sentence those who commit criminal acts here on the Rez."

For the first time in his memory his grandmother interrupted him. "Mo, I know all that. I know the tribal courts work under the jurisdiction of the FBI and have only limited powers. But why was Ernestine's case sent to the tribal courts? Why didn't the FBI come in and investigate the rape of a young girl by a vicious and dangerous man? Federal agents should have been here, Mo. I am not blaming you, but now the FBI is responsible for the death of my brother."

Mo reached over and took his grandmother's hand, trying to explain the FBI's priorities. Alberta was very unhappy.

"What their priorities say is the value of an Indian's life is not very great. An old man like my brother is hardly worth

95

bothering with, even if he was murdered by a repeat offender who may go out and kill again." Alberta shuddered. "And what if he comes back?" The question hung in the air.

I listened to Alberta talk about injustice. She was incensed on my account as well as her brother's. She was unhappy with the inadequacy of the system. She cared about me. She considered me a granddaughter. The reality of that almost made me dizzy.

My grandmother—my father's mother—never called or tried to contact me in any way. She knew where I was, where we lived. The murder of a famous hatathli made news across the reservation. She'd told me over and over again she was too old to raise a child. It was true. She was too old and she had been for many years. She just couldn't take any more sorrow in her life. She used to make me angry, but when Billy died I couldn't hold on to any more hurt. She was doing the best she knew how and I had been fortunate afterall. I had my family.

Now sitting at the table we had our very own FBI agents. Maybe they could make a difference. In an informal way Mo began to question family members.

22

Gathering facts

Helaman waved me over to the table. John and Lucy pulled up chairs, ready to talk to Mo. "Why are you sure it was Tsosie?" Mo asked in his soft voice.

John held up a finger. "First, and to me most important, my father was killed with a rock. Tsosie could have used a knife or a gun, but he chose a rock. It was retribution—payback—for the shame Tsosie felt when an old man knocked him down with a rock." He held up another finger. "Also, my father saw a gray blue sedan pass by the house in the mid-morning."

He held up a third finger. "And Ernestine," he nodded in my direction, "saw Lewis Tsosie with a gray blue sedan at the trading post in Kaibito about noon. Fortunately Tsosie didn't see her."

Helaman took up his part of the story. "We were on our way to Page headed to class. Cell phone service between Page and Kaibito is spotty. But as soon as we got to the school we ran into the computer lab, looked up the number for Chinle Correctional and I called. They told me Tsosie' was released on November 20th. They didn't bother to contact Ernestine or our grandfather. I guess that's part of the system too. Anyway, we called and told grandfather to get out of the house. He already knew Tsosie was coming. Your father doesn't miss much," he added with a nod toward John. "Ernestine and I thought he would leave the house. He reassured us; he said everything would be fine. He was just going to wait for Delbert." Helaman stopped talking.

"Did you see his car?" Mo asked.

Helaman shook his head.

Mo spoke to me. "Did you notice the plates on the car?"

I nodded. "I wrote it down on my notebook. I didn't even think about it after we got back and found everything." I paused not wanting to put my thoughts into words.

"Can you get the plate number Ernestine? It might be a help," Mo still spoke in his soft voice.

John picked up the conversation while I went to look for the notebook. "Lewis Singer is the lead officer on the case. He told me the admissions clerk at the Med Center over in Kayenta remembered a fellow coming in early Wednesday asking for an address for the hatathli, claimed Billy was his grandfather. He gave her two names, and she gave Singer a pretty good

98

description—tall, skinny, weasely face. Long, black hair. It fits Tsosie," he added and everyone smiled.

"All she had in the records was that he lived in Shonto. Tsosie must have talked to somebody over here." John cleared his throat and looked at his son. "When Delbert got to the house his grandfather told him to stay inside and take care of Little Billie who was napping. He was real emphatic that Delbert was not to go outside for any reason."

Mo looked over at Delbert. "I stayed in, but when I heard the noise outside I peeked out the window and I saw a tall, skinny man bashing in . . ." J Tears filled Delbert's eyes. ohn reached over and pulled his son close.

"Delbert saw it all. He saw the same blue gray sedan Ernestine saw at the Spirit gas station and he saw another man sitting in the car."

"Another man?" both Mo and Nicky asked surprised. This was news to them.

"Yes, a second man with Lewis. He must have been the one who killed the dog. He knew the dog wouldn't let them get close to the house." John's voice dropped almost to a whisper. A well-trained sheep dog is like a member of the family. They would mourn the loss of the dog. It was another blow, a second loss.

Nicky spoke up, "Does anybody know who the second man is?"

People shrugged and looked at one another.

I came back in with the license plate information and John paused before continuing. "Here's the thing. Officer Singer and Officer Dishface are good at what they do, but we don't want this murder to be prosecuted by the tribal police. We need the FBI to come in on this, Mo. All of us agree

99

with Alberta.

Mo looked at John. "I can hardly believe what I'm hearing. Everybody on the Rez hates it when the FBI comes in and takes over a case. They don't know the area, they don't know the people, and they don't understand our language or traditions. Nobody trusts the FBI. Nobody talks to them."

"All you say is true. But the tribal courts don't have the authority or the leeway they need when it comes to sentencing." He repeated what had already been said, "Lewis Tsosie was given a two-year sentence for assault and rape. He was given the maximum sentence the tribal court could give. We want justice. We want a fair sentence for this family and for our father. Mo, can't you come and investigate? You're FBI and Dineh. We trust you. We don't want a big team making a lot of noise, but we want Tsosie tried and sentenced by the feds. We want him to spend the rest of his life in prison. He is an evil man. He came back here when he should have walked away. If there is no penalty he will kill again."

"I understand. We all want the same thing, but even if I can get assigned to this case, even if I can get the FBI to consider it, I can't come in alone. I will have a team too." But Mo couldn't walk away. "If it is possible I will come here in an official capacity and investigate. I have no official status yet but I have some questions. Who did Tsosie talk to in Shonto to get the address for the house? Is anyone looking for the Chevy sedan,? And how do I get in touch with Officer Singer? Once Singer traces the plate number we may have another important piece of evidence."

I listened to your Uncle Mo as he systematically began to take control, and I felt hopeful. Maybe the monster would not walk away again.

23

Dog Eat Dog

Mo Black did talk to the FBI. He was assigned a team and authorized to investigate Billy's death. Fortunately I was not involved. I went back to school, commuting with Helaman, doing homework, focused on my nursing degree. Lucy agreed to look after you while I was in class. John suggested that I stay with his family until Tsosie was apprehended, and I was glad because it meant you would still see Delbert almost every day. Lucy was glad too. Delbert had been through a traumatic experience. He had nightmares, but in the afternoons he could let go of the horror that haunted him, sit on the floor and play. He could be a kid still. In just a few years he would start junior high. He might have to act like a tough guy then, but that could wait. In the evenings I worked with Lucy in the kitchen, but mostly she and John simply allowed me to fill the role of a big sister in the house, a big sister with a busy class schedule.

Once in awhile Helaman would mention something he'd heard about the case. Occasionally I would ask if there was anything new. Lewis was wanted for the attempted murder of a woman out near Shiprock—his own mother it turned out. He was involved in the murder of a woman in Gallup. He or his accomplice had shot a DPS officer. Somebody heard the men were Skinwalkers, shape-shifters. I shuddered and hoped they were gone.

Helaman assured me that Lewis and his traveling companion did not have the wherewithal to be Skinwalkers. It would have required them to study and learn the Navajo Way. Those two didn't have the discipline or the inclination to study. They hadn't been raised in the traditional way nor had they acquired such knowledge in any other way. To turn medicine to evil you have to understand good medicine. Still there was plenty evil out there for them to find.

In mid-February we heard that Lewis and Leon Nez (his accomplice had been identified) were spotted up near Aneth, Utah on the northeast side of the Rez. I hadn't realized how tense I'd been but on hearing the news I felt my body relax. They were out of the area at least for now. Weeks passed with no more news.

Soon the semester would be over. Thank goodness I had my classes. I was busy studying, working to keep my grades up, and it kept me from worrying. It kept me from thinking about what had happened and what might happen.

And of course there was Helaman. As much as my classes helped, Helaman helped more. We still drove to school together. We studied together. We ate lunch together. And we talked, sometimes about school, sometimes about our lives, and sometimes about the future. Some evenings on the ride from Page to Kaibito I would find my eyelids drooping. "Hey Ernie," (he was the only one who called me that) "lay down here on the seat. You can use my knee as a pillow."

"Some pillow," I retorted. "I might as well find a rock to lay my head on." I stopped. I couldn't go on. I'd been making a joke and it had turned back on me. I saw Billy again lying on the ground, his head broken.

Helaman looked at me. I must have turned pale. He pulled over to the side of the road. "Ernie, Ernestine. Look at me." He reached out and touched my shoulder. I let my forehead rest on the passenger window. "Ernie." He moved over and took my chin in his hand.

I looked up at Helaman and saw devastation in his eyes. He felt responsible for my sorrow. Neither of us had words to heal the hurt. It lay deep inside at my very core, but I could see that I was not the only one who suffered. I wasn't the only one who loved Billy.

I leaned forward, and now my forehead rested on Helaman's shoulder. My arms reached up around his neck and he pulled me close. Holding onto him I felt the pain diminish in the warmth of his embrace. He kissed the top of my head, my hair. He laid his cheek against mine and he held me. I don't know how long we sat together without speaking.

Finally Helaman sat back, looking down at me. His voice was husky. "Ernestine Yazzie, I love you and I will take care of you as long as we live. "

I looked up at Helaman, wide-eyed. "Is that all you can offer me, just a lifetime? Helaman, I'm going to be with you forever."

Helaman started laughing. "All right, if that's what you want, you've got it. Let's plan on forever."

On Friday evening Helaman dropped me off at my little car behind the Spirit station. He watched me unlock the door and start the engine. I waved and he waved back as he pulled out. I turned southeast on the highway headed for Shonto. It was past twilight moving toward the full dark of night. It had been a good day, a busy day. I'd had practicum all day. I was working in the hospital under supervision. Mostly I changed beds, took vitals, smiled at patients, patted hands. But it was satisfying.

My head was buzzing with thoughts of the day. The headlights cut a tunnel down the dark road in front of me. As I came around a bend a coyote loped across the road and entered the light from my headlights heading southeast. I braked and turned the wheels to the left, veering out of my lane. I was focused on not hitting the coyote and not driving into an oncoming vehicle, not like there were a lot of vehicles on the road. I felt the adrenaline pounding in my veins, and I congratulated myself. I had swerved and missed the coyote. I had given myself plenty of space. I was safe and my car was intact. I pulled back into my lane.

Everyone knows Coyote is a trickster. He may appear to be a friend, but at any moment he can turn on you. You must be careful with Coyote. When he travels to the south or east he may be trustworthy. But when he travels to the north or west he travels toward darkness. A Coyote headed toward darkness

104

is dangerous and definitely can't be trusted. He can't even trust himself.

As I straightened out the car I looked ahead. A scream escaped my throat. Coyote had turned to the north and was running toward the front of the car. Yes, Coyote is a trickster, but this time the danger doubled back on him. I slammed on the brakes, staring into the yellow eyes on the road in front of me. He looked huge. He stopped directly in front of the car, paralyzed by the light. He stood teeth bared, the fur on his hackles standing straight up. I was going to hit him. I was too close to swerve, too close to miss.

For a moment I thought I could stop in time. I thought Coyote would turn and run. But instead he lunged at the car, a howl cutting through the night air over the sound of my engine and squealing tires. I felt the bump and suddenly the animal was gone from sight.

Shaking, I pulled over to the side of the road. No one knowingly crosses Coyote's path. Even the school bus driver stopped and waited for another car to come down the road, to cross paths with Coyote before continuing on his way. No one knowingly crosses the trickster. But this was different. We had collided, that coyote and me.

I waited for a minute or two before opening the car door. The coyote was lying on the road twenty feet in front of the car. I walked to the trunk and pulled out a shovel. Armed with my shovel I walked up the road. I have to tell you I was afraid, very afraid. I thought of all the stories of Skinwalkers I had ever heard. What if the coyote was still alive? I could still see the snarling mouth, the bared teeth of just moments before. I thought of all those things, my hands shook, but I moved forward. Finally I stood looking down at the animal. He was

105

dead, there was no question of that. And laying there on the road the coyote looked small. He looked diminished. He could no longer hurt me.

I stood and thought about that coyote and about Lewis Tsosie. Lewis thought he had the power of Coyote. But he was wrong. He was just a bad man. I had killed this coyote and I didn't want to leave him on the road. I would have to use my shovel to move the carcass.

The animal was still warm, steaming in the cool night air. I pushed the shovel under the body and half scooped half scooted the animal off the road. I walked as far as the closest juniper tree and dumped the carcass under its low branches. Let the crows and coyotes find him. Let them pick the bones clean, pull the eyes from the sockets, scatter the bones.

Standing alone in the dark I felt a power I had never felt before. Maybe it was adrenalin, maybe it was understanding. I smelled the sharp scent of juniper where I'd disturbed the branches. I remembered the smell from the Enemy Way; from the white soup Mo and Nicky drank to purge the evil inside. I reached out and crushed the juniper needles between my fingers. I smelled the strong, pungent smell on my hands. And I knew. I was clean.

I walked to the car and dropped the shovel in the trunk, slammed it shut, and began to sing one of Billy's songs. A sense of power filled me, a power I cannot describe. The monster was dead. When I dumped that coyote off the road Lewis Tsosie was dead to me. It hadn't happened yet, but I knew it would I knew that like this coyote his carcass would be left to the crows and the wild dogs. The monster was gone. He could not hurt me. He would not be back. He had no power.

Sitting in the driver's seat I felt a lightening of my entire body. It was a very real physical sensation. I seemed to be floating. At that moment I could have flown above the car. I remembered riding in the back of the pick up with Sunshine and Pearl and Rachel so long ago, back in a simpler time. I remembered how the wind had pulled at us, how light we had been. Now, sitting in the car, I felt that same sense of elation. *I am no longer a child; I am a woman*, I realized. *I am a grown woman who will do what it takes to protect myself and those I love.* There are defining moments in life, moments that can make a difference between life and death, between walking in beauty and stumbling in the dark.

24

White Shell Woman

Helaman could turn almost anything away from darkness back to light. He was such a joker. Not a trickster, he was truly funny. He had something everyday to start me laughing. He was better than a big brother, he was better than a cousin, he was . . .? What was he? I couldn't find the word I wanted. I just knew I didn't want to think of life without Helaman in it.

Driving into Page on Tuesday Helaman pointed out toward the west. A beautiful rainbow filled the sky from north to south, sparkling in the light of the early morning sun. "White Shell Woman must be visiting," Helaman remarked.

I looked out at the rainbow. The sky looked white with the brightness of the sun, a perfect day for her visit. I looked back at the rainbow and I thought of While Shell Woman. I was glad she had come today. Today I could tell Helaman about they coyote.

I straightened up on the seat, "Helaman, I killed a coyote Friday night. It ran in front of the car before I could stop."

Hclaman looked at me with conceren. "Why didn't you tell me yesterday? Are you alright?"

I smiled. "I was waiting for White Shell Woman. I wanted to tell you at a moment just like this."

He looked at me, puzzled.

"Helaman, I killed the coyote. I left if for the crows and dogs. It is dead and gone. And now this morning White Shell Woman is here with her promise of protection and hope for the future."

Helaman nodded. "You are a brave woman Ernie, and White Shell Woman brings powerful medicine. She comes with the rainbow and the March winds whispering messages of hope in the ears of those who listen."

I smiled. "I'm glad she's here. She brings us the sunshine of safety, the power of dreams, the beauty of hope. That is what she's brought today, hope and the power to overcome."

Billy had taught me the stories of White Shell Woman. Would she keep her promises even to me? I thought about that for a moment, and I knew the answer was yes.

Helaman pointed to the rainbow, "Do you see that golden eagle right there flying over the rainbow?"

I leaned forward and studied the sky, but I could not see an eagle. "Where is it, Helaman?"

Helaman laughed. "I don't see it anymore. I must have been blinded by the light. He turned toward me. "Oh, here it is." He was smiling.

What are you talking about? What's here?

"You are Ernie. You are my White Shell Woman. You bring me the promise of hope. You even have a little golden eagle." He meant you, Billie. You are our little golden eagle like White Shell Woman's companion.

"But White Shell Woman went off and lived alone," I said to Helaman, shaking my head. "That is not my way."

"She wasn't alone," he countered "She had a husband and her golden eagle. And with me she never would have left," he teased. We both laughed.

"I'm not going anywhere—spring, summer, winter, fall this is where I want to be. We can take care of each other. I'm not White Shell Woman, Helaman. I am just Ernestine. But I know White Shell Woman came today to bless me with a healing way and she came to confirm what I already knew. The monster is dead."

I accept her promise for the future, Billie. I live with hope. I walk in beauty.

25

Gone to the dogs

That same week Mo and Nicky came back to Kaibito. Somebody had seen Tsosie east of Montezuma Creek. Mo hardly stopped. Singer was waiting for him in Kayenta and somewhere over in the Utah corner of the Rez two monsters were waiting for justice.

Instead of parking at the Spirit station I drove out to the house and spent a few minutes visiting. I smiled at Nicky. "Helaman told me you and Mo are expecting. Congratulations."

She beamed at me and put a finger to her lips. "It's

true, but Mo would kill me if his parents find out before he gets back."

I nodded. "I can keep a secret." Nicky's smile grew even wider if that was possible. "Yeah? Then I'll share another secret with you. Helaman told us you two are getting married after he graduates next month." She watched my face and started to laugh. "Shouldn't you act surprised when he proposes."

I threw my arms around Nicky's neck. I had to hug somebody. "I'll tell him I'm not surprised. I caught him at the War Dance and he never paid to get away. He's mine." I started to laugh. I hadn't thought of that before, but I knew Helaman would laugh too. "I just hope he doesn't wait to long or I'll burst."

We didn't hear from Mo for several days and then he was back. When he walked in his face was grim. Nicky, Esther, and Alberta ran up to him ahead of everyone else. Nicky spoke for all of us, "What happened? Did you get them?"

Mo shook his head. "The FBI won't be prosecuting Tsosie or Nez. They won't be getting that long prison sentence we were looking for."

"What?" Everyone was stunned. "What happened? Did they get away again? Why aren't they going to trial?"

Mo shook his head. "No trial. They were given a death sentence, and it's been carried out."

Alberta stumbled back into a chair. "Thank you, God," she whispered. Then she looked at Mo. "Did you kill them?" There was concern in her voice.

Mo shook his head. "No grandmother." Then he told us the grisly story of Lewis Tsosie's demise. Lewis and Leon had spent several weeks in Cortez. They holed up in an abandoned building, kidnapped a young woman and laid low.

I shuddered knowing things must have been bad for the woman. Mo told us what he knew about Sally Dawson. "Lewis put a choke chain around her neck and attached a cable to it."

I feel my throat. I think of Lewis's belt looped around my neck, how he pulled it tight cutting off my air when I tried to pull away from him. I think of the burns on my skin from the leather pulling against my neck. Sally was chained up for days. I imagine the scars left by the chain. I don't want to think of what else she suffered.

Mo is still talking, "Fortunately, Sally managed to escape from the predators. She was a brave woman, she feared her captors were insane, and her only hope of escaping alive was to literally escape. She ran barefoot through snow and ice to get away from her tormenters.

"When she escaped the two men realized their hideout was no longer safe. They fled back into a remote area on the reservation looking for another place to stay. Eventually they came to an isolated valley and moved into a chindi hogan, a hogan abandoned after someone died inside. Lewis and Leon rustled sheep and tried to tan the sheepskins. They were trying to harness Coyote's power. The smell at their camp attracted wild dogs. It didn't take long before people began to talk. There were missing sheep or dead sheep in scattered corrals. One man spent the night out with the sheep, ready to protect them from predators. His brother found is body the next morning. Rumors of Skinwalkers circulated. But even with the rumors no one could find Tsosie or Nez.

"Then a woman out riding on the mesa top spotted smoke rising from the abandoned hogan. No Navajo would enter a chindi hogan. She talked to her brother and he called

113

the police."

Mo and Signer went out to look into it with Tso, Zuñiga, Sims, Dishface, and Boyce—the whole team. By now they were pretty sure they were on the right track. They came to the creek below the hogan after dark, waiting so they could approach unseen.

Mo stopped at this point in the story to explain, "You know we were all a little leery of these two. Tso spotted the men and he whispered to me to be careful. He whispered right into my ear mic from up on the mesa. Then I looked up and saw the Flint Boys in the northern sky. There they were, the friends and protectors of Monster Slayer and his brother. I felt so happy at that moment I almost laughed out loud. We couldn't lose. There we were five of us creeping forward in the dark and Tso and Zuniga up on the mesa top directing us with the radio. Me and Singer, Sims and Dishface coming up behind and Boyce hanging back at the rear. And there in the sky were those stars." Mo paused, overwhelmed by emotion. "The Flint Boys, two up high, two in the center, and three coming behind, one lagging. Some things are beyond explanation, beyond conscious planning, but I felt their power and protection. I was one of seven good men and we were going to stop the monsters. Grandpa Billy, our Monster Slayer, was up there too, watching, making sure Tsosie and Nez didn't get away."

Helaman leaned in. "So what happened?"

"They heard us. We yelled at them to come out. They yelled back. Lewis told me he'd already killed Monster Slayer. They came out of the hogan. I thought we were going to arrest them, but we hadn't counted on the dogs."

Esther's hands flew up to her face. Everyone on the Rez knows stories of dog attacks.

"While we were moving up from the creek the dogs were moving across the bottom of the mesa. They came forward suddenly, thirty or forty dogs surging toward the men, surrounding them in waves. The dogs howled, Leon howled, Lewis wailed. We shot at the dogs, but they were in a feeding frenzy. Well. You get the picture."

I didn't say a word. I knew when I killed that coyote. Some things are beyond explanation. We sat in silence until Alberta spoke "We get the picture. We got justice, Reservation justice. Thank you, Mo."

26

Finding Beauty

Helaman and I were married in August. The family gathered in an outpouring of love and support. I looked out at the good people surrounding us and I remembered the words Alberta had spoken to me at Billy's funeral " You don't know much about death. Your heart is still young. You must learn how to be strong; you must carry a vision inside you. Look at the world as though you were looking not at the next mesa, but ten buttes away."

Alberta had paused. "Those are your grandfather's

words," she added almost as an afterthought. Then she went on, "Great evil happens at times in this life, but it brought you to us and it brought us Little Billie. It brought us all great good. Look forward daughter."

There are things that happen in this life that hurt and keep on hurting. The death of Billy Gray Eyes was not one of those things. Billy was the kindest, wisest person I ever knew. But despite the loss we felt I knew he had died to protect us. He had died so that evil could not win in this world. When I think of Billy I know how much I was worth to him—how much he valued all of us, and I hold my head higher because of him. We were lucky. In the end evil destroyed evil. Billy told me one time that was how things are in the world. Those who follow the Destroyer get caught in his trap.

But Billy taught me to walk in harmony.

My father was right when he told me each family begins a new world. I hope our new world will be a place of peace and justice, a place of happiness.

Great evil happens at times in our world, but I have you and you have me and we have Helaman. We are a family and we must create our world together. We will stand against evil. We will walk in Beauty.

Remember and look forward daughter. Look forward.

Thanks

Thank you for adding White Shell Woman's Promise *to your library. I hope you enjoyed reading this story as much as I enjoyed writing it.*

Now that you have finished my book, will you please write a review on Amazon or on GoodReads?
Reviews are the way readers discover great new books.

If you enjoyed *White Shell Woman's Promise* be sure to look for *Monster Slayer's Son*, a companion story to *White Shell Woman's Promise* also set in the Navajo Nation.

You may also enjoy *Down the Colorado, Sparrow Hawk* and *Up the Devil's Highway* in the Kiko and Maggie Perez series.

Also look for my book *Shaman Priest*, set in Guatemala,

Contact me at: carmencomments.wordpress.com
or on Facebook at: facebook.com/karen.hopkins.731

Made in the USA
Lexington, KY
17 December 2016